W9-CAH-874

The Voyage

Also by Murray Bail

Fiction

The Drover's Wife and Other Stories (1975)
Homesickness (1980)
Holden's Performance (1987)
Eucalyptus (1998)
Camouflage (2002)
The Pages (2008)
The Faber Book of Contemporary Australian Short Stories (editor) (1998)

Nonfiction

Notebooks 1970–2003 (2005)
Fairweather (2009)

The Voyage

Murray Bail

MacLehose Press

MacLehose Press
An imprint of Quercus
New York • London

First published in the United States by Quercus in 2014

ISBN 978-1-62365-072-8

Library of Congress Control Number: 2013937922

Distributed in the United States and Canada by
Random House Publisher Services
c/o Random House, 1745 Broadway
New York, NY 10019

Manufactured in the United States

2 4 6 8 10 9 7 5 3 1

www.quercus.com

The Voyage

IT WAS NOT SO MUCH A HEADLONG RUSH FROM EUROPE, MORE a slow return to Sydney, instead of hopping onto a plane, which would have been easier, Delage had chosen to return by ship, not one of the P. & O. queens, a container ship, stacked with the rectangles of various faded colors, which stopped at half a dozen ports along the way. On the ship—it was called the *Romance*—he imagined there would be silence. Not total silence: of all people, the specialist manufacturer Delage knew there was always a sound of some sort, however faint, even an echo, somewhere. One of the attractions for Delage was there would be just five other paying passengers. A priest who was supposed to join ship at La Spezia had canceled. Delage would have a cabin to himself. Aside from the occasional "Good morning!" and an occasional "Thank you," he was looking forward, after what he had been through, to thirty-three days of peace without talking about himself, or having a significant conversation of any kind. Most things are not worth saying, yet continue to be said. What is said is a version in a different voice of what has already been said (many times before). From the moment Delage stepped onto European soil and began speaking or spruiking, he became aware his voice was only adding to what had long been there. The dark trees, the streets and boulevards, the clothing of people and the expressions people arranged around their mouths, even the air they breathed, were blurry or furry with the accumulation of words, congestion in the guise of world-weariness. You would think they might have been interested in the views of an outsider, one who had come from the opposite direction, literally from the bottom of the earth. But no, not really—even though, unencumbered by tradition, the New World had a history of throwing up new methods, the fresh solutions. No, they showed little or no interest, preferring to remain standing in the one spot. In Vienna, in particular, to just about everything he said, these exceptionally neat, implacable figures with almost unworldly tanned faces, from skiing recently in the Alps no doubt, almost clashing with their silver hair, remained smiling, while some even, the women, kept their blue eyes on him and began laughing. They knew their Mozart, Beethoven and Brahms. How many times would they have heard the "Jupiter"? Strauss used to come around to their houses and play the piano in the paneled drawing room. Before long they would casually, almost dismissively, recall personal anecċes about poor Schoenberg. The daughter of one of them, Elisabeth, who he met at a soirée—spoke excellent English—took him the following afternoon to a street behind the cathedral and into the apartment where

Mozart composed, among other things, "The Marriage of Figaro." As he climbed to the first floor, Frank Delage realized Mozart's feet had actually been on these very steps, which were quite worn. The rooms had loudly creaking floorboards and a few bits of fragile furniture, allowing visitors to see nothing more than the space in which Mozart and his family moved and the view of the street he undoubtedly enjoyed from the main window. To Delage's surprise, Elisabeth had never been there before. She had been born in Vienna, and therefore into music, everyone in her family, the von Schalla family, listening and playing and nodding in time with it; naturally she assumed he too was music-saturated, like everybody else in Vienna.

The very nature of his invented product meant he could not ignore Europe, a "vital plank," as one of his investors said, with a serious expression. And by normal commercial standards his foray against the ramparts of old Europe could hardly be called a success. At the very least he hoped to have one foot in the door; now, with both Vienna and the possibility of Berlin behind him, he wasn't even sure he had achieved that. Already he was thinking he might have to go back! If he did, or even if he didn't, he decided he was going to talk less. It was something he had learned from the implacable Austrians, the Germans too, for that matter. There was something wrong with people who never stopped talking. Away from home, Australians like to be chatty, not that anyone anywhere thinks or cares about what they say. He himself was not a talkative person, not normally, but in Europe it had been necessary to make headway with the locals, somehow. To Elisabeth, he hadn't once mentioned the word "piano." After the Mozart museum they went to a coffee house behind the cathedral, where she talked about her family, the Schallas, as if he knew of them, reserving her perplexed emphasis for her father. In fact, when you added it up, it was she who did most of the talking. In reply, Delage described his sister in Brisbane, who, he said, phoned often three, four times a day. Either she rattled on about nothing really, or complained about a situation way beyond her control, such as the unseasonal wet weather, or else she would report progress in her self-appointed task, even though it was hardly her concern, trying to find him a wife, or a "possible wife," as she put it. "My sister could talk under wet cement. She has psychological problems, as far as I'm concerned. She has to spill it out. She has to hear herself talk," he explained, just off the Graben, in the city where it had all begun half-horizontally on Berggasse, the confiding endless sentence. "There's obviously something wrong with her," he went on, wanting to rub his eyes, although he knew there was nothing wrong with his sister. "She'll talk about anything that comes into her head. We're not like each other at all." Put them in a room and they didn't even look like brother and sister. "What's her name? Jo—short for Joan." In sympathy, Elisabeth pulled a face. The only thing of interest Delage could remember his sister saying was in response to their new stepfather, "He eats too much jam." Talking is alright, as long as it makes a difference.

It's best not to release thoughts immediately. Isn't it best to pause? An added benefit is that it gives the impression the person is being thoughtful, accordingly someone worth listening to.

It was one of those sensible conclusions he had reached long ago, but hardly ever put into practice.

Frank Delage carried around a notebook for jotting down things he had read or heard, the way some people pick up cigarette butts, they could end up being useful one day, not only maxims, although most of them were, unusual phrases, descriptions too, he liked the sound of single words. A green fountain pen protruded at the ready from his shirt pocket, which also pointed to energy, a range of set tasks to be tackled. "Let me see," Elisabeth, of the von Schalla family, said, and began flipping through the pages. "The human face is the most interesting area on earth"—one of his favorites. He had forgotten where he'd come across that one. "Thinking remains thanking." Somewhere else he'd picked up a description of a rubber band "the color of a nun's belly," which he had immediately written down, even though it didn't give any advice at all. It was enough for Elisabeth to tilt her chin, as if she were resting on her elbows on a beach, and give a small laugh, not entirely unaffected, for it revealed to Delage the pale curve of her Austrian throat. Elisabeth was in her mid-thirties. Good of her to drop everything to show him, a stranger, around Vienna. Obviously she had the means, and plenty of time on her hands, she could do whatever she wanted. Every time he glanced at her or asked a question she was looking away. He had filled many notebooks. Such a need to retain the thoughts of others suggested Frank Delage was undecided about himself, that he was composed of little more than the thoughts and opinions of others. On one subject he had clear and confident thoughts, where he knew what should and could be done, and whenever he talked about it he never borrowed the words of more articulate, stronger people. On this subject, Delage, the manufacturer, could be tenacious, sarcastic, indignant, intent on demolishing, or at least reducing, the opposing forces. It was a remarkable product, his, in every way an example of New World ingenuity. For many years it had consumed his energy and money earned or borrowed, mostly borrowed, leaving little or no time or money to be directed elsewhere. At forty-six, still with plenty of dark hair, Delage lived alone, as his sister needlessly pointed out, although he was not necessarily lonely, he had become a diffident, distracted sort of man.

"Have you noticed," she said on the third or fourth day, "the motion of the ship draws words out of us. Words that I, for one, would not normally say?" He was conscious of the linen sleeve on the rail, almost touching his.

All around were hills and valleys, about waist high. The sea was busy mimicking land. It was all charcoal, desolation, everywhere. To the woman the lines of foam kept dissolving into trails of lace. I could look at this all day. It was the sea, said to be soothing. And from a depth far below, as if in a mine, the power of the great long engine came up through the plates of the ship, trembling the rail and numbing most of her toes, her feet in sandals appeared unusually soft and irrelevant on the metal deck, the sandals gold with a narrow raised heel, dainty, inappropriate, although bought specially, the ship, despite its name, having no decoration of any kind, let alone softness, everything cut or cast from steel and oversize, nuts, bolts, levers, hatches, chains, rivets the size of dinner plates, an all-steel masculine complexity. What an engine: no stopping, day or night. Delage generally took an interest in, or rather was alert to, mechanical surroundings. If asked, he could probably explain most of the parts, although the window on the bridge sloping in at an angle left him baffled. The superstructure and rails were white, everything else the ship's owners had painted a lurid matt orange. "Imagine what their lounge rooms in Hamburg must be like." If Delage had said something like that to the woman standing beside him, a woman of taste, inappropriate gold sandals notwithstanding, she would have rewarded him with a woman's laugh, which had its conspiratorial aspects. There is the constant male instinct for slipping into humorous or even clownish mode to please or divert a woman's thoughts. At any moment it will happen; it was one of Elisabeth's expectations, acquired early on. With little trouble her father could make her laugh, never her mother. Of course it can lead to embarrassing awkwardnesses, faux pas, and "lead balloons," as they are called, of the most inept kind, quips or puns that miss the mark, make no sense, are too obvious, or are repeated once too often, while irony hardly ever works; and still there is the need in men to continue—clowning for women, pulling faces, being plain silly, often falling flat, it doesn't matter. A certain carelessness is allowed. For the woman, it lightens the endurance required in dealing with the heavy, persistent presence of men. Delage here said nothing, the woman turned from the sea, and smiled anyway. She was out on the ocean, in safe hands, a warm breeze touching her cheeks, seabirds coming from somewhere, swooping over the ship. "Don't say 'boat.' It's what the Americans say. This is a ship." In Vienna, she went about with the casual authority of the resident, while on the ship heading for Sydney she was in the hands of others, "all at sea?" Delage suggested, though not seriously, where every part was a mystery, hard, thickly painted, moving forward, slightly unstable.

By detaching the three tapering legs of the company's demonstration model, and having it quilted and professionally crated, Delage could carry it on board as accompanied baggage, his small manufacturing company on the outskirts of Sydney, consisting of eleven uncomplaining employees, craftsmen most of them, always looking for ways to save money. It was the bookkeeper who had spotted the luggage loophole. She was Slovakian, an exceptionally neat, unsmiling woman, in her forties, stranded after her no-hoper husband had gone back. At the job interview, she had offered to work for nothing, or just the basic wage, "because, you must understand, I believe in music." Delage had to be careful here. Many of those who choose a career in medicine, because they believe in doing good, turn out to be the worst doctors imaginable; and politicians who have the good of the people at heart are invariably ineffective—just as people who love art too much have no idea what is a good or bad painting, and end up with a motley collection of too many paintings, none of them worthwhile. But the Slovakian bookkeeper had quickly attained complete mastery of the job, simplifying the systems and so on, finding savings in the most unlikely places, and managed to put the impatient banks back where they belonged. She was called in and out of board meetings to clarify figures, until it became her habit not to wait outside but to sit on a stool against the wall inside, smoothing her short skirt with short nervy hand movements, ready to pipe up with answers to any questions. Delage wasn't the only one to wonder how they had managed without her, although, as he told Elisabeth, of course no one person is indispensable. When he described her tantrums, including ultimatums, hands over her ears and pencil-breaking, which more or less tracked the sauntering amateurism in the office and factory, Elisabeth wanted to know more. She was interested in another woman's hysteria? At the same time, she didn't appear to think her behavior so unusual or extreme. They were on the *Romance*, standing together on the small deck, facing a breeze over and above the movement of the ship. From the moment the bookkeeper took her place in the office, Delage went on, and established herself as the first to arrive and the last to leave, it was assumed she had no life outside work, until one morning, after she had been looking unwell and rushed into the bathroom, it was proclaimed quite calmly by several women that she was pregnant. Only then did Delage recall seeing her one night in a pub, well away from the factory, sitting in the corner with the apprentice who had large red ears, who must have been at least twenty years younger. "So," said Delage, realizing he might have been talking too much, "that's our highly prized bookkeeper. Thanks to her money-saving talents, here I am—sailing on the ocean, a lot of time on my hands." "Did she have the child?" Elisabeth wanted to know. "Not yet. I mean, not as far as I know." He had arrived in Vienna with introductions to people of influence, and he needed to win over at least one of them to have any hope of succeeding in his cause, even if success meant not outright rejection, but a pause in the long-established European assumptions, the way a single arrow can clear the wall of a castle under siege, and produce a barely perceptible but spreading ripple in the ranks of the defenders. All he had to do was to arrange a demonstration—after first pointing to the radical construction of his concert grand piano. Logic would surely take over; they would see the point; from logic and mechanical efficiency came the distinctive new sound.

Soon after he arrived Delage stepped out from his hotel and took note of his surroundings, which offered no clues, except that he didn't have warm enough clothing, and back in his room he set to work, scattering papers all over the bed, telephoning, e-mailing, drawing up lists. So much for these personally recommended contacts! Many of them were no longer alive, had actually died years ago, even the concierge could have told him, while others had moved to more progressive musical centers, Berlin, Amsterdam, or the broad pastures of the United States, while those remaining had placed themselves out of reach, at least initially. These were the managers of the concert halls and the all-important conservatorium, as well as the most influential piano teachers and, Delage had been warned, the music critic for the main daily newspaper, a Bertolt Brecht lookalike, who also made a point of not shaving or bathing regularly. Either they were too busy, or they couldn't be bothered, whatever his importance in his particular field (no-one had heard of him); and when the personal assistants to these managers and piano teachers realized he didn't have a word of German, some of them turned downright rude. All he needed was five minutes of their time, it wasn't much to ask. After pleasantries, five minutes would flow into another five, him talking, explaining, not taking his eyes off them. If it became too technical, he'd notice and change tack. It was not possible to do it over the phone. It had begun raining, Vienna darkened still further, straight out of *The Third Man*, when he went out with a list of addresses and a tourist map, and ended up taking directions from a salesman in the Steinway & Sons showroom, who actually came out onto the street and pointed in the opposite direction—a demonstration of over-confidence, if ever there was. At each office he didn't get beyond the outer office or antechamber, where he was left to wait on various wooden chairs, creaking along with all the floorboards of Vienna, the loose joints of conservatism, as he saw it, the chandeliers, lamps with tasseled shades. "I hardly got one foot in the door," he told Elisabeth. "They would have been happy if I'd sat there twiddling my thumbs for years." In one of the music schools, he could hear a piano playing, and gazing up at the decorated ceiling he wondered why and when anyone would paint in each corner a pale blue cherub blowing a horn (representing "music"?) and soon he began to wonder what he was doing there, in

Vienna, in Europe. Not far from the hotel was the Café Griensteidl, a comfortable place where Delage sat and waited; prodding at a strudel with a fork went with examining his lack of success in the city, that is, whether it was all to do with him, something in his personality, his way of almost deliberately going about half seeing, of not at the last moment bothering, and how he did or didn't get along with certain people, in fact most people, now that he thought about it, even back home. What sort of impression was he giving? He couldn't be sure. There is a general unhelpfulness among Europeans, as if a mass of severe experiences has kept them one level above the small things, above weaknesses, the slightest of separations but enough, not that their recent history was anything to be thrilled about, Vienna being one example. If it hadn't been for his innocent energy, a sort of cleanliness in the face of indifference, he might have cut his losses, packed up and gone home. It can't be that difficult. He almost said it aloud. It's only a place.

Delage had an engineer's mentality, although he had no training or diploma in engineering, more an inventor's mentality, directed toward a single specific mechanism he had happened upon—the restless inventor attracts good fortune. He was a man who easily became engrossed; and, as if he was looking up from solving a problem, he had developed an oblique way of seeing people and the nearby world. His sister was forever saying his mind ran too much along a man's lines, that he'd be a more interesting person, he'd have more friends, if he included in his thinking a woman's way of thinking.

Women, she said, he told Elisabeth, are attracted to a man who has a woman's psychological conversation, that was the word she used, "conversation," and the layers of affinity it produces. "It's the combination. Interesting," Elisabeth began to nod, not getting it quite right. He liked looking at Elisabeth, or more often, glancing at her. Here she was holding on to the rail with both hands, facing the breeze, an advertisement for expensive sunglasses. With the rushing sea below, Delage couldn't avoid calculating his chances if he had the misfortune of falling overboard, the shock of landing in the deep cold water, legs kicking, nobody noticing as the fat stern slowly disappeared. "Do you agree with what she said, your sister?" Elisabeth had turned. Before stating the obvious, which was that his sister was always on the phone, giving firm advice, just checking up, as if he was in need of help, he said, "By way of example, she said I should take an interest in fabrics, their colors, the feel of them." Every conversation is an exaggeration. A story told, a description, voices imitated, an idea or a thought put into words, they're condensed or colored—tailored—to hold the listener. And Delage was constantly aware of doing it himself, anything for the stronger effect, especially when leaning forward and selling the virtues of his remarkable, as it had been publicly described, invention, the Delage (piano). Women waited for attentiveness, they allowed even the most shameful exaggerations. Was that what his sister, Elisabeth too, apparently, meant? In conversation, Delage had noticed he avoided a woman's eyes, it was unnerving the way they frankly met his, unwavering, nothing in the world to feel awkward about, at least when talking to him, the receptionist at the hotel the most recent, instead, he had formed the habit of glancing away at something, the corner of a table, or a bird on the wire, or the traffic passing, and so missed the effort, what appeared to be the truth, behind the face. For all his difficulties with the eyes, Delage, when drawn into a psychological conversation, felt a shifting of interest to a more personal, intimate level; and he felt part of him flow to the woman, and back to him, the bookkeeper, he recalled looking up from her pristine desk in Sydney, now Elisabeth. They had the subtle grasp of situations.

Every other street had a shop devoted to music, their windows displaying recordings of the most acclaimed performances, as well as the most recent performances, which of course is not the same thing, while others specialized in sheet music or books on music, busts of the greatest of composers, now made in China, conductors who couldn't help composing, and vice versa, wind instruments in the window, and one offered second-hand violins (and violas). The calculating businessman in Delage, the most irregular part of him, wondered how they all could make a living. You would think by now every family in Vienna had its piano or music stand, not to mention the alabaster bust of Beethoven on the mantelpiece. And yet Steinway & Sons had at least two dozen concert grands in their showroom, and probably more out the back. Near the Albertina, one shop had a cluster of metronomes working in the window and a display of white plates which featured around their circumferences a pattern of black keys as seen on a piano, so that someone eating their sausage and sauerkraut would be encouraged to think musical thoughts, perhaps even to hum a few bars, in particular, piano, as they wiped the plate clean. A woman in a cream coat splayed at the hips and glossy cream high heels was talking to the owner, who glanced at Delage and went on talking. He was selling these "piano" plates, but showed little respect for those who bought them. At the same time, Delage couldn't help but notice, he was listening to and smiling at the woman, as if she were known to him, the thin and tall (as well as bald) shopkeeper tilted toward her, pressing one hand to his waist, the other cupping his elbow, as if he were in severe pain, which made him appear, in every sense, lower still. Turning now, speaking to no-one in particular, except she seemed to appeal to Delage who happened to be in the shop, she switched to English. "What to get a man for his seventieth? A husband is an impossibility." Delage saw she had on a small, very smart round hat with a remnant of a veil, like a piece of delicate graph paper, called in more accurate times a "fascinator," something Delage didn't know, which shadowed her forehead. "A husband who has most things, I would suggest," the shopkeeper widened his smile. "A piano," Delage joined in, not even seriously, "a new piano." Her face was accustomed to giving the quick glance. "He has more than enough pianos." "Yes," the shopkeeper glared at Delage, "of course he has pianos." The shop represented in miniature the reception the city had been giving him since he arrived. "I know of something your husband couldn't have, couldn't possibly have. There's one in Vienna, as we speak. It's under wraps. Would he—but, first of all, you—be interested in something modern? I don't think so." Delage could hear himself sounding forced—too formal. A sudden change in circumstances, and voice and manner can change, whereas a simple awkwardness can be more truthful. At the door he gave a bow to both of them, which probably looked ridiculous, and out on the street he remained for a moment in full view, deciding whether to go left to the Griensteidl, or right to the hotel, or cross the street and head toward the gardens; after all, he had nothing better to do. The color of her coat and shoes was the same lacquered cream as requested by one of his earliest customers, a piano to match his wife's hair, perhaps that was what made him look twice, so he was thinking, when close by she spoke, "You've taken that poor man's plate." Delage saw it in his hand, and made a move to hurry back in. "Leave it. He won't mind. Tell me, in there I did not understand what you were talking about?" There was nothing worse than talking or explaining himself, his presence in Vienna. "This was for my sister, who lives in Brisbane. She has a cupboard full of plastic Eiffel Towers and Statues of Liberty, and what-not, places she's never been to. This plate she'll like. She'll put it on the mantelpiece." The smallest thing could make his sister happy, or at least happier, she'd be on the phone to him immediately. He'd post it somehow when he got back. Close up he saw around her eyes the beginnings of softly radiating lines, helped along by the Austrian skiing season, "crow's feet" back in his dry country, but it only made her more elegant. "Do you have a brother?" he asked without warning. Meeting a person for the first time, Delage invariably spoke abruptly, almost harshly, which was odd, for he didn't look harsh at all, the instinct was to ward off, even for a minute or two. He went on, "I find this is an unimpressive place. I mean the city itself. By the way, you looked completely out of place in there. I can get you a taxi. I'll do that." He stepped out onto the street. It wasn't necessary, the shopkeeper could have told him, Amalia Marie von Schalla had her dark limousine and chauffeur waiting by the curb. Shop for the tourists, "piano" plate, sister, local woman wearing little hat turning to leave: another second or two and the rapidly intersecting lines would not have met (had Delage remained staring at the display of plates in the window, instead of stepping inside). Moments of chance break into the flow of everyday life, producing aftershocks, sometimes deflecting a life for the better, or worse, so common that a subsequent once-in-a-million, so-called stroke of luck or a complete coincidence should not come as a surprise. The lost ring, a slip on the ice, wrong number, taking the wrong seat, bumping into a stranger, the flight missed, the right place at the wrong time, stopping to tie a shoelace, do I know you? At the window seat at the Sacher, she had the over-casual manner of giving time to someone, Frank Delage, she would normally not be bothering with, certainly not over coffee, such as it is in Austria, and the world-famous Sacher pastries. The headwaiter had elbowed his three waiters aside to greet Amalia Marie von Schalla, and found a table when there didn't appear to be one by snatching with a histrionic flourish a small printed sign "Reserved," and was excessively formal to the elderly American couple who arrived almost simultaneously, the man red in the face, "Now you listen. I'm room 401, and a booking was made seven weeks ago," etc., it went on, the difficulty of remaining neutral in a foreign city. Amalia von Schalla took her time removing her gloves, and seemed to ignore or give only the faintest acknowledgment to similarly gray-blond women in their fifties at other tables, craning to have her attention, while at the same time, Delage could not help but notice, examining him, the strange man accompanying Amalia—they cannot help themselves. "I see women here like to wear hats indoors, but I haven't seen one nearly as special as yours." Men too went about on the streets in white raincoats down to their ankles like laboratory coats, local fashion, apparently, therefore hardly worth mentioning. In a low voice that had him leaning forward she went back to his speech on the footpath: "In many ways I would agree. Vienna can be difficult. But you are suffering from frustration. You cannot be expected to know our city." To rest his hand on her hip he leaned back at a somewhat awkward angle on the sofa, smelling of her and her skin, a yielding woman, for in her softness she continued to take an interest in him, even though she could sit without moving or speaking for an unusual amount of time. Elisabeth pondered the answers he gave, now and then repeating a word in English. "Talked about this and that. She was easy to talk to." Elisabeth moved her hair to behind her ear, and spoke in a dreamy sort of way, "She's not like other mothers. I could tell you plenty about her." "I think it was what I had to say about the piano situation, in general. She took an interest. I thought that was pretty unusual." In turn, he managed to keep his eyes on the face before him, on an angle. For all the wealth behind Amalia von Schalla's elegance it did not appear as a deliberate elegance, which only draws attention to the effort, little more, and was a large part of the envy of other women believed to be her friends. "She has always liked clothes," Elisabeth said, after a pause, "and you have seen the house." "What was your mother doing in that shop? I meant to ask." Twisting around, Elisabeth lay herself across his lap looking up, which broadened her cheeks, almost the face of another person, her breasts too fell away, the breasts of another, happy for him to survey her paleness, her wide openness. The different voices, expressions, movement of shoulders, her pauses and sudden opinions had become part of her appearance. "Am I too heavy for you? Tell me if I am." She remained looking up at him, his hand on her belly, "You're not listening. What happened? Have you told me everything?"

And it rained on the ship, everything became slippery, they stayed in Delage's cabin, a sofa, brown floor, metal desk, the small double bed. "I am not complaining"—gave his arm a little punch. The von Schalla houses in Vienna and Upper Austria were more like warehouses for oil paintings and furniture, cavernous corridors and galleries, the small drawing rooms where elderly servants crept in and out, the many details of lavishness spaced out to impose themselves, as required. He had seen her father's desk, how it swarmed with scrollwork, entablature, gold-leaf flourishes, which had crept in from the city's churches, its theaters, seat-of-empire buildings and fountains, leaving hardly enough room for a sheet of quarto, von Schalla's legs barely fitting underneath. Behind his head, a vast gold-framed mirror by a trick of perspective forced Frank Delage and any other visitor to be conscious of their distant positions. It was from this small desk that Konrad von Schalla, short, blue-eyed man, had directed his and his wife's considerable fortunes into chemicals and made a chemical fortune, soon followed by a cement fortune, and built up from the same tiny desk a European-hotels-and-theme-park fortune, and on meeting Frank Delage he took the opportunity to make off-hand inquiries about the Queensland cattle industry. Through the portholes, other ships and Mediterranean fishing boats appeared as horizontal colors, dissolving in gray. "You are thinking maybe I'm soft," Elisabeth sat up. "I would like you to know, I've camped out in the high forests. What do you know about snow?" Sometimes it is a matter of leaning back and not saying anything, not even smiling. Acceptance can be encouragement, it can be done by remaining quiet. Aside from a few piles of snow, the one subject Delage had, more or less, mastery of was the piano—inner workings of, unaltered (as if it was the best we could do) over centuries. Leave out the knowledge of the revolutionary construction of the Delage, its fresh sound appreciated by a few adherents, and his life was mostly blank. Until recently it had been difficult to think clearly about what was there, now it felt as if he were being led—to some area where it would be better for him, a small distance, but away from what he was beginning to sense himself to be. "I told your mother about my family. She wanted to know where the Delages came from." "Delage" had an aura of Europe and European craftsmanship,

Benson or Cook or poor old Jones would simply not go with a piano, "the Benson piano," or "the Cook piano," or "the Jones concert grand," it would not work, whereas the Delage was there on the lid in serifs and repeated in product brochures, invoices, business cards, signage, clearly a piano backed by a long tradition, look at the name and the serifs, even though the Delage Piano Company in an industrial suburb outside Sydney was barely fifteen years old. "In the 1920s, there was a car made in France called Delage," he told Amalia von Schalla, "I think I am related." At this she laughed. "Have you properly looked into this? Can you be sure?" "It was known as the French Rolls-Royce. That's good enough." The information had come down from his unreliable grandfather, the wool-buyer all the way from Lyon, on his first visit fell for a Sydney Rocks barmaid, never went back, he told Amalia von Schalla at the Sacher, while she recalled that her grandfather had owned a Delage, or some name like it, powder-blue, with maroon upholstery, in contrast to the other old families who remained loyal to the silver Mercedes. Seated there, Frank Delage could not escape the thought that if Amalia von Schalla as a young woman sat in the maroon leather of the Delage, she would have been sitting on him. His father, Sydney-born, a screen printer and a mason, did his best to neutralize the atmosphere which surrounded "Delage," he referred to their second-hand Vanguard as "the Delage," and at every opportunity liked to mock the fancy French, or Frenchness, or foreignness of his name, pressing it into common usage, instead of saying "large," saying "a delage piece of that cake, if you don't mind," or, "these trousers are too delage for me," and other such nonsense, and gave his son the name Frank, plain and practical. At their first meeting, Delage did his best not to come across as an obsessive, not wanting to be the Jehovah's Witness who has the black shoe in the front door, or the Mormons in the drip-dry shirts, their neatness and cleanliness illustrated the promise of paradise, ready with their tedious answers to every question, every objection, drab unhappy people, never feel sorry for them, at the same time it was necessary to describe the mechanical features of his new piano to explain why it produced a superior, or at least a different, sound; and when Amalia von Schalla showed patience and apparent interest, and ordered another round of the Sacher's excellent pastries without even a glance at the waiter, it was easy for Frank Delage to believe he was not obsessive, not at all, but a person who had arrived with a possibility, and for a moment or two could keep talking with his mouth full. A person can go through an entire life without having a conversation with another person, nothing to show over the years than thousands of murmurings and mutterances, the distracted nodding, not entering, not taking part, so missing what waited within the other person—"the accumulating curiosity," Delage had noted from one of the English newspapers at the Griensteidl. Changing position to have her back more to him took the weight off his tingling arm, sending it more or less unguided over her shoulder to drape, he was talking about her mother, to her breasts, first one, the other, a drape which has the feel of ownership, had he wanted it. "I have carpenter's hands, look. But all I do is walk through the factory, shouting instructions to everybody. That's become my life, looking over shoulders and pointing out expensive bloody mistakes." The morning he'd had to snap his fingers in front of the apprentice for falling asleep on the job! Across the table, her hands remained alongside the suede gloves, a pair of fixed crimson shadows almost parallel to her hands. "I want to say, if this piano is so good, why is it you do not have an agent selling it for you? We have piano agents in Vienna. Why do such work yourself?" "Good point. That should be the next stage." "It requires local knowledge"—she straightened her gloves—"which you do not have." The local product enjoyed the home-grown advantage of manufacturers' names polished darkly by the legendary pianists in thousands and thousands of concert performances, not only across all of Europe, in the Americas, Japan, Australia, New Zealand too: the Bösendorfer piano, the Bechstein, Faziolis, a long succession of Steinway & Sons. Now add the Delage (Sydney), Delage said, though he did not actually come out with the words. "Each in its own way a Mount Everest. Do you have any idea?" In Vienna he had to keep reminding himself, do not get into the technicalities, people are not interested, even if he was interested, it's too difficult, and anyway not the point, all a person had to do was sit down and listen to his piano being played, notice the different tone, cleaner, there was one under wraps in Vienna, transported from Sydney at enormous expense for the very purpose. At first he thought Amalia von Schalla was one of the best listeners he had come across; on the other hand, the attention she paid to his ambitions may have merely been the habit of aristocracy which made her "come down" to a conversation, just as the Queen of England is said to be wonderful at dispatching all sorts of onerous tasks, at the same time being a most wonderful conversationalist. It wasn't merely a new person revealing themselves. Across the starched table in the Sacher, she seemed to stretch and become taller, her lines became straight lines, more alert, more of a presence, to the point where Delage wondered what there was about him that could possibly interest her. "Oh, I have a free day," she said, after shaking her head at the exaggerated stories about his family (sister), the harbor city, man-eating sharks, his knowledge of music, of old Europe, "unless you have somewhere else to go." But diffidence ran deep in the family, it was seen as a virtue. Frank Delage's father went around with a permanent wince, as if he had been punched in the stomach, turning his wife still more inward, protected by the walls of the kitchen, it was she who insisted on a piano and lessons for their son Frank, there biting the bottom lip, now sliding his eyes from the faces of women in case he was caught—ordinary male shyness, or hopelessness, widespread in Sydney, even more in the rest of Australia—and when, as in Vienna, circumstances made it necessary to depart from this inherited shyness, Frank Delage managed it awkwardly, departing too little or too much. Coming to Vienna had not been a wise decision, there had to be a better way to introduce a revolutionary new piano. Habits develop which become part of what we are, difficult to change, "pianists and conductors, concert promoters are amongst the worst," ticking off points on his fingers, at the same time not wanting to appear relentless. "The composers keep on inventing, or reinventing, and there is some sort of progress in science, I'm told, while the actual playing of music is stuck in the mud, coming out with the same old sounds." By way of agreement or to cool him down she reached across with a napkin and removed a flake of pastry from his chin, the advancing shadow of a stout woman, large nose, small eyes, tan feather in her hat, seemed to pause before enveloping the table. "Amalia, can we expect you tomorrow?" Without turning, Amalia von Schalla introduced Delage, "I think we need to call you an inventor. Clever man. He has come all the way from Sydney. Tomorrow evening, yes." To Delage, "Berthe will have some people it is important for you to meet." The large woman glanced at Delage, "Thank you, Amalia, thank you." And later, after Delage finally succumbed to the technicalities of what gave his piano superiority, describing the shorter distances of the hammer movements, the different surface of the hammers, the different frame and hardwoods used as a consequence, these were real improvements, and of an unexpected kind, only then after listening carefully, or appearing to, Delage all the while managing to keep his eyes on her, more or less, she didn't mind, she accepted perhaps even understood his gaze, did she suggest lunch the following day or perhaps the day after at the Hotel Bristol not the Sacher, by which time she'd think about what he'd said. Elisabeth had placed her hand between his legs, "My mother and father had nothing more than a business marriage. I still cannot work them out. I do not know that I ever will." The pregnant bookkeeper's thrift had forced a delay in Delage's departure, which allowed Elisabeth to join the *Romance* at Piraeus, although she could have caught the ship farther on, at Port Said or Singapore, for example, Delage was stepping down the corrugated gangway thinking he might walk into Athens, a city he had seen so often in photographs, or at least the noble ruins of it holding up against the blue sky, always perfect blue sky, along the streets he would observe the many local customs, he would take his time—from the top of the gangway he saw Elisabeth looking up, expecting someone to take her three suitcases. The ship had been left unattended by the German officers and crew who had piled into taxis heading in different directions for the brothels. When he told Elisabeth, she said, "But aren't they married?" The sky was thick with clouds, the sea dark, almost black, it rained, it stopped, rained again—pelting the ship as it passed through. In the Mediterranean, Delage expected to be amongst lumps of land broken off what is called Greece, white stony islands everywhere, the ones which appeared here in the rain blurred into the color of half-submerged legs and shoulders of lamb. "Please don't look surprised. You know what I'm like." Against the stained concrete of the wharf, a gantry began to move, Elisabeth appeared as paleness and softness, well satisfied with her decisiveness, already a success, Frank Delage trying to fix a smile, although it only revealed a confusion, he knew, he hardly knew her, Elisabeth von Schalla, not in three weeks, not nearly enough time, although from the first word at the soirée he had liked her, Elisabeth of the Schalla family, and went down to carry up her suitcases. "What have you got in here?" They weighed a ton. Also she brought her own pillow made of goose down, the pillows in a cargo ship would undoubtedly be hard, if they had any pillows at all, away from home Elisabeth was always accompanied by her pillow filled with goose down, even having it under her arm entering the best five-star hotels, a display of feminine sensibility Delage almost admired and she ignored. "I told you I was coming. And you decided not to believe me." "Your mother, does she know about this?" "You left in a hurry"—although she wasn't really cross, it was too interesting being on a ship. The epaulettes on the dress gave her a faint Germanic touch, there is still the military residue, diminished by the thin yellow belt, and a small maroon lizard- or crocodile-skin handbag, which added to her gaiety. The ship bulged and shifted against the wharf, straining to depart. And yet he had had every intention of keeping to himself, settle the thoughts, to gather them, as people used to say, he was "gathering his thoughts," going over what had happened in Vienna along with what should have happened in Vienna, sliced across by a tram, how he had responded to each situation and so on, what he should have said and done, but had not, instead had done something else. To do this it was necessary to be alone, not easy on the ship, on any ship. From La Spezia he had spent hours leaning over the rail following the waves, the five other passengers he looked upon at meal times with careful politeness, making the smallest conversation, little more, before returning to his cabin where he stretched out on the bed, or sat in a chair, all the time aware of the ship driving forward; now Elisabeth on board would require him to talk, take an interest and so forth. It is difficult anywhere to do nothing but think, it's difficult even to gather thoughts, it is more and more impossible to be clear, there are too many alternatives, Delage had always skipped from one thing to another, a "grasshopper mind," father liked to point out, just as it is impossible to remain in a stationary position anywhere on earth without hearing a sound. Delage was shown to the table at the Hotel Bristol, Amalia von Schalla arrived late, she tugged off her gloves, a different pair (different suit, speckled blouse, no miniature hat with fascinator), briefly acknowledged his presence. It had been her idea, her invitation, now she was unhappy over something nobody else had a clue about, perhaps she wondered why she was seeing him again, at the Sacher sipping coffee, while he ate the pastries, she had got on too easily with him. And here he was again in his one-and-only two-button suit, from a faraway place she could not imagine, a tall open-faced man who looked as if he should be missing a front tooth, a salesman walking the streets of her city, knocking on doors (unsuccessfully), if it had been hardware, or boots made from kangaroo hides, not something to do with music, a piano with a revolutionary new sound, she would not have given him five minutes, let alone lunch at the Bristol. "There's also a car called Bristol," he said, leaping onto yesterday's conversation, for he believed it had been a success. "I've seen a purple one driving about in Sydney sometimes. They were built by an airplane company in England, and made special use of aluminum." At the mention of "aluminum," Delage thought she would walk out. "Aluminum!

Do I need to know this?" Her shoulders rose and fell. "Whenever I think of this hotel, which I should say has been a favorite of mine, I'll now think of a piece of metal." "Haven't lifted a finger this morning but read the papers. I wrote a few letters—business letters, the usual stuff. Now I am all yours." "I do not need you to be nice. Thank you. If you don't mind, stop now. I prefer here to the Sacher, I do not know why. I seem to have grown up in the Sacher. We become hostages to habit—who was it said that? There is another place I could have taken you to. They specialize in chocolates. You know nothing about Vienna, I keep forgetting." Once again people at various tables recognized her, Amalia Marie von Schalla, and gave little waves. The simultaneous eye, finger and silent mouth movements are deployed by women in public to bridge a gap, while actually keeping the person at a distance, a function of some importance, apparently, for it has not been diminished at all by natural selection, if anything it has been strengthened. It surprised Frank Delage to see how it was followed by comments only partly disguised by the backs of hands, or out of the corners of mouths twisted by lipstick. Gradually, Amalia von Schalla began listening again, aware that the artists and composers, no doubt the inventors as well, rarely came from her aristocracy, but were thrown up by the restless, ever-hopeful middle classes, and deserved respect of some sort; he began looking at Elisabeth openly, following her contented movements as the ship went forward, it pushed ahead at a constant speed, the resistance, she could feel, strolling about in his cabin, casual, chatting away, naked. From an overnight position of losing interest in Frank Delage, beginning with his insistent physical presence (a practical eye-shifting alertness, sometimes it made him appear canny, although she didn't believe he was), along with the repeated specifications and superiority of his new piano—he'd invented and built with his own two hands—"necessary breakthrough" not piano, he preferred, which of course had no hope of making an impression in Vienna, the most musical of cities, not in a thousand years, "necessary breakthrough" or not, Amalia von Schalla could see, now passing her hands back and forth from her cheeks into her already handsome blond hair, repeatedly like a carpenter shaving curls of Huon pine, she returned to taking an interest in him, when she certainly didn't have to, in his energies which began in his face, precise, alert, at the same time an almost careless set of energies as if it was all in his neck and arms. She listened closely as he launched an attack on the senility of Vienna, of the hidebound, dreary musical establishment, all parts permeated by the fossilization of old Europe, all the old countries, the old states, "and England is no better," the Tudor cladding, complacent, head-in-sand, tedious places, and still the superior airs, still laying down the law, what a joke; Europe wasn't aware it had lost it, slipping down and farther down over the years, "historical has-beens," and actually made worse by music, in particular the violins, the blurry cellos, not to mention the never-ending ballroom waltzes, or "schmaltzes" as he called them, giving a layer of honey over the ordinary present, Vienna the worst. There was quite a build-up of pressure out there. Mild-mannered pianists have been known to lose it and bang their foreheads on the lid or break their big toes kicking the legs, he said in an approving way. "That would not happen in Vienna." "Why not? It's not too late to be modern," he told her. And although Delage had been perplexed by her change of mood he returned the fork to the plate with a slight rattle ("F sharp?"), and invited her to see and hear the only Delage piano in Europe, "worn out, over-decorated Europe," a fresh piano sound to be demonstrated to her, only her, Amalia von Schalla.

"My mother is a handful at the best of times. She is not a mother out of the textbook. When I think about it, she was hardly a mother at all. I do not know what she was thinking. She would have no more children, she said to me. I was more than enough for her. She always had to be somewhere. If it were not for music, she would have gone mad, or something." As she lay across his lap talking about her mother, the ship was going farther and farther away from her mother, quite a distance already, although still in the Mediterranean, the last of the Greek islands, as Delage had stroked her mother's healthy blond hair, their farewell in the room, he thought of this as he stroked Elisabeth's shorter hair, traces of her mother's broad forehead, eyebrows, upturned mouth below him, even their breathing was similar, yet little interest in music; in that vital area she and her mother were opposites, he looked ahead to arriving home, to The Delage piano factory at the industrial edge of Sydney. He had sold just the one piano in Europe. Sunlight came through the porthole: a white egg shape lit up on the brown floor, enough for Elisabeth to reach down, very languid, to show her hand illuminated. Before she, Amalia von Schalla, could hesitate, or say no, would rather not, or that doesn't sound like a good idea, consult her watch, or we have not yet had our coffees, Delage stood up and took her hand and raised her from her chair—who else had done that, in the last twenty years, and in public? "Come along, let's have a look at the dangerous instrument everybody here wants to run a mile from. Don't come, of course, if you'd rather not. I'd like you to come. And you don't have to say a word." For a moment, Amalia von Schalla's composure in the dining room was even more regal than usual, until spreading to a slight smile. Her mouth was not at all thin and hard, which can happen as a woman grows older, even when she has no disappointments, or only a few. In the back of the limousine he realized he knew virtually nothing about the woman beside him, about the Schalla family, their position in Austrian society and Vienna's musical world in particular; had he known he may not have invited her to the demonstration in a warehouse. At that stage, he didn't know she had a daughter, Elisabeth, it hadn't occurred to him to ask, he hadn't asked many questions at all, absorbed as he was in the task of introducing his piano. "We are an old family, one of the oldest. It has its disadvantages." The interior of the limousine was almost feminine in its spectatorish leather softness, impassive bearded chauffeur up front, not wearing a cap, a bodyguard a possibility, Amalia von Schalla seated as if she were at a music recital, a restrained restlessness which was repeated or emphasized by the cut of her suit and blouse; alongside such intentional elegance—finely tuned, successful—Delage began to have doubts about his piano, whether it measured up, whether his claims for it were true, or true enough, whether in the end he had been wasting everybody's time in Europe, including his own. It was odd that he hardly knew the woman seated beside him, Amalia Marie von Schalla, as they drove in her limousine toward his humble piano, a mystery woman who remained very still, but seemed to be taking an interest in the streets they passed, as if she had never seen them before. When he tried to recall another woman who showed even one of Amalia's minor characteristics he drew a blank. The driver was leaning forward, looking out for the address, Delage at the different styles of architecture and other sights. The old buildings, industrial, older than anything in Sydney or at least different, carved stonework above the windows and doors, left him feeling out of place, it would be difficult, it already was, the factory in Sydney (its tools and equipment, leases, capital owing, telephones, office chairs—they had an Italian espresso machine) and his staff, who at least took notice of him, were far away, while here the heavy unwelcoming city went about its business, even down the side streets, his presence not making the slightest difference, all of which increased his doubts about the new piano. Stopping and reversing, the chauffeur said something in German, swearing, Delage assumed. There was too much clutter in his life, he could see, small objects, the blank spots in between, a life of stumbles, of heading in a general direction, people close by, only a few within arm's length, one or two, reasonably energetic still, all of it leading to the piano now up and running, a piano of possible importance, but that was all. It was what his sister had been alluding to for years. "Hey! I've forgotten to shave. That's not like me." "So you have"—a different smile from her, one side of the mouth. They had left the car and crossed the street, Delage taking her arm, into an office where a man with red hands sat at a desk, a crucifix on the wall above, Amalia von Schalla speaking in German, "the Delage piano from Australia," the man led them through the office, along a corridor, another door, and switched on the lights. A mass of seabirds had settled on the water, a floating pattern rising and falling, as if to music, the fluorescent lights stuttered and finally came on full, revealing to them, looking down from about half a dozen concrete steps, a sea of pianos, black, wall-to-wall, room for not even one more, similar to contemporary artists who fill a gallery floor with nothing but thousands of small standing terracotta figures, or arms from dolls, or broken chairs, or hair, or artificial eyes (or shoes, or arranged on the floor small photographs of men from a poor village somewhere, and even one gallery space in Berlin filled with nothing, just wall-to-wall air), an initial shock through incongruous exaggeration, momentary, banal if considered for a moment, but gazed upon with reverence by gallery visitors, a profound experience for them, such is the necessity of diversion, the seabirds flew off to form another pattern, to the left the glossy black mass of concert grands was broken by one under calico, hidden under wraps. "Spot the Delage. Which one do you think?" Again he took her arm, finding a path through the pianos in storage, the great names shoulder-to-shoulder in polished head-of-state limousine black, which had them all looking the same or similar, easy to become lost among them, it was necessary to advance sideways in order to squeeze a way between them, until in from the left they reached the one under wraps, found a space, more important a stool for her, where the magician or the shark from the Antipodes assumed the posture of a showman, made a ridiculous trumpet fanfare with his mouth, believe it or not, anything to amuse her, a woman, his awkwardness due to the circumstances, in a sudden movement whipped off the dust-sheet. The sight of his piano, the first to arrive on European soil, made him wonder if he had been away from Sydney for too long. Crowded out to one side by the regimented black of the European concert grands, the Delage was revealed as nicotine-brown, the color of a bantam rooster, and stood out accordingly. It was like his cousins from the sticks the year they'd gate-crashed a family wedding in Sydney, wearing loud neckties. This was what he was up against in Vienna! Already there was enough prejudice against the interloper without color becoming a factor. Black, as in piano, represented depth of feeling, before even a single note was played. Nicotine-brown—what did that represent? The Delage Piano Company produced most of its pianos in jet-black, the most popular choice of buyers, he wanted to say, maple, oak, Huon pine were some of the timbers used, yet the same company, his, was staffed by thoughtless bludgers who in their thoughtlessness, general slackness, their casual amateurism, send one of the pale brown (with inlaid mother of pearl) models by mistake, obviously a mistake, a color of piano which may have gone down well with buyers in southern Queensland, or parts of the Middle East, but not in Vienna, the music capital of Europe. Delage had his arms folded, looking down at his shoes which were parallel to a crack in the concrete, and noticed one of his laces undone, the difficulties ahead, the piano's future, his future and the factory's future, still without turning he gave a "tomorrow's another day" shrug, which was how Amalia von Schalla read it from behind, his optimism or resilience, one or the other, or even both, not, she saw, a man given to moods. "What would you like"—lifting the lid, "Chopin, George Gershwin? You choose." Before she could answer, he sat down and began playing honkytonk, rapid, loud, improvised, hardly appropriate under the circumstances, completely inappropriate, as a matter of fact. Not only did the color of the demonstration model lack the necessary depth, the choice of music and Delage's hectic playing, switching without a pause to other tunes, did not match the occasion, the moment, Amalia von Schalla of all people, what was he thinking?, unless it was his way of expressing disappointment, or washing his hands of a fiasco. And straightaway the sound was cleaner, sharper than the normal piano sound. "The hammers travel a shorter distance," came the explanation, still with his back turned. "As a result, there's less vibration of the strings." He struck a middle C again and again, expressing frustration aside from anything else. "Why anyone would bother to play an old Steinway," he shouted over the playing, "is beyond me. They're a load of rubbish. The old pianos get away with blurry notes, you can hear the hammer bashing away at felt, not like this. You hear the difference? The old pianos are stuck in the old sound." He moved in and out of Liszt and Lara from "Doctor Zhivago," and finished by flinging out an arm and throwing his head back, in mock homage to the virtuoso who continues to play the Old World pianos, as he put it, which was when Amalia von Schalla saw he had mismatching socks. The man was not a good seller of goods, the advantages of his product were self-evident to him, and there were as well the many years which had gone into perfecting his piano: his signature there in a gold flourish above the lid, which produced in her a strange feeling of pity. Amalia von Schalla was drawn to gifted men, especially those involved in music or art of some sort, for if anyone could properly understand her it would be one of them, perhaps only them. Taking her hand was to be expected, she allowed it, other gifted men had taken her hand, although she looked past him, Frank Delage, to the yellow-brown piano. "Do you know, I am beginning to like it. It has an interesting quality." In a fit of eagerness, Delage dropped her hand, "What? Not the color, surely?" With her head to one side she continued the appraisal. "It would not look out of place in drawing rooms in Vienna, let me tell you." Since there was bad taste in abundance at every turn, including the ornate preferences of her own husband, an otherwise austere man, the glossy piano made in Australia from pale timber would fit in without difficulty. Entire apartments were decked out in pale tables and chairs, touched up with gold. Chandeliers were a feature, even in cake shops and hair salons. And amongst Vienna's endless bric-a-brac, men of all ages, in fact men across all of Europe, had taken to wearing enormous attention-seeking watches on their wrists, as if watches were jewelry and men should decorate themselves, a frightful lapse in taste that has left many shaking their heads. After he replaced the dust-sheet, careful to tug it down at the corners, almost forgetting her as he carried out the task, another man would have flung it over and left it at that, she observed, drew her to him after he straightened his back, a simple movement the way he pulled tight the dust-sheet, and took a freedom he didn't understand but allowed anyway, her cheek, to her breast, which waited for him, its soft warmth filling his hand; the density of the pianos in storage prevented him from finding, out of the corner of his eye, a place hidden from view, on top of which was the fluorescent lighting, before he realized she could not escape, grand pianos close behind and to the sides, giving the impression, an entirely false impression, he had trapped her, forcing himself upon her, a woman must be allowed space to slip away. Although watchful, wondering what would happen next, Amalia von Schalla was reassured by the eyes which remained close to hers, no ice in either one, khaki, her husband's clear blue beginning on her wedding night. By then his hand had fallen away, "Very good of you, it really was. Who else would come here? Anyway, so now you've heard it." Amalia von Schalla wanted to laugh, disheveled, even if she knew there was not a hair out of place. "You are grateful to me?" "Of course. By that I mean—" "If you could only see yourself, you're red in the face." At this point Delage would normally cough, or come out with a quip, or crack some sort of joke, anything to deflect the attention, although here he chewed his lip at what expression to adopt, solemn, jovial, modest, an appealing awkwardness, up to their waist in pianos, she not so much looking at him but surveying him. The door above the steps suddenly opened, metallic, followed by a harsh gurgling voice, which could have been an order or a question, enough to trigger in Delage a newsreel of crouching soldiers, tanks, black smoke, dead horses, old women wearing head scarves. "He says he has to lock up." "My concert is over, and just when I was getting warmed up." At last she threw her head back and released her face, she was less regal, new vertical lines formed from the mouth down, how the beauty of some women increases with age and laughter, and looked away. The deck, such as it was, had a steel floor painted brick-red, which interested Delage—so much metal surface in the world!—as he leaned over the rail, his elbow touching her sleeve, knowing her hardly at all, everything she said was new, the way it was said especially.

In the evening at an apartment on Karolinengasse, twenty to thirty people would have been standing under the chandelier said to be the largest and heaviest in Vienna, a city which has developed a chandelier neurosis, more cut-crystal chandeliers in Vienna than any city on earth, and so the spread of subtle artificial lighting, sipping champagne, chatting about this and that, pairs of women angled on apricot-colored settees, a few smokers, not a word of English, at least Frank Delage didn't pick up any, to one side wearing his thin suit, waiting for something he could relate to, not even from the waiters who had exceptionally smooth skin and stiff necks. He reached out for another glass as a tray passed. Elegance was important to these people. Much of it came from the immaculate state of their clothing and hair, the men especially. When he spotted Amalia von Schalla, who wore a silver dress, glittering as if lit up by electricity, she turned slightly, no more than a millimeter, enough to move out of his field of vision, and continued talking to several people at once. Delage wondered what he was doing there, she had scribbled down the address in the car, perhaps wanting to do or say something after what had occurred in the warehouse, touching his hand with a fingernail, "people will be there," whatever that means. It is impossible to know what another person is thinking, it is difficult enough to know what we ourselves are thinking. In the piano warehouse, Delage didn't know what her thoughts had been when his hand had—automatically—moved to her cheek and breast. In another room a piano and cello were being played. "Your name is? Amalia said you would come, and you did. Good. Let me introduce you to some of these wonderful people. On the phone Amalia reminded me you are from Sydney, not a place I have been to, unfortunately, and you know everything it is possible to know about pianos and their construction. Am I right? Even if only a speck of that is true, you must be very clever." Frank Delage recognized her from the Sacher, Berthe Clothilde, large perspiring nose, which cried out for an oriental diamond, small eyes, not as slender as her friend, Amalia, sharp inquisitive manner, by extension the long single rope of large-diameter pearls she continually twisted around one finger, while bobbing about below her throat a vintage brooch of a peacock, all gold and filigree (wings), its tail erupting like a fan cooling her throat. "It is a musical evening. Next month—it will be architecture. Or is it Islamic pottery? It doesn't matter, there is much to learn. Are you with us for long? Look at Amalia. Where would our poor little Vienna be without her? Everybody wants to stand close to Amalia. There won't be any room for Konrad"—glancing at Delage—"her husband. Excuse me." The hostess stepped forward to greet a short man in a bulging black T-shirt, and a young woman with wild orange hair, wearing a transparent black blouse and various chains. Pierced lips, eyebrows and so on, streaks of color, paint thrown over their faces and hair, appeared in the early evening in parts of Sydney, and even other cities of Australia, as well as across Europe, England too, small outbreaks of flamboyant conformity, Delage felt around for his pen and notebook. Everybody had drifted into the adjoining room where the cellist and the male pianist continued playing, a Steinway, Delage noted, of course, an apartment with its own music room, its own Steinway concert grand, next to it a harpsichord, its ancient lid closed, mercifully, as far as Delage was concerned. The inadequacies of the harpsichord created the piano! The harpsichord had a bucolic scene on the lid, some sort of German custom, Delage assumed, cavorting nymphs, the distant castle etc., and so on, Old Europe arranging the scenery even back then, which gave Delage the idea, he made a note, paint a scene of native trees, eucalypts, on his piano which would rear up into a forest when the lid was raised (notes flitting like birds through the smooth trunks?). If not to everybody's taste it would at least declare where it was manufactured, a graphic reminder of the differences between his piano and the antiquated, established pianos, he needed as much help as he could get, from anywhere. He also wrote in his notebook something he had read in a newspaper, "All the same in our differences." Or words similar, he'd have to think about that. Chairs had been arranged in rows, the men continued talking in a subdued manner, women sat expectantly. The cellist had the human-shaped instrument between her legs, giving birth to difficult music, the pianist who wore a white skivvy kept glancing across at her, the hostess, Frau Berthe Clothilde close at hand, waiting patiently for them to finish. There was nothing for it but to continue listening. Delage half turned to the blond woman who had taken the seat beside him, "What is it they're playing?" not expecting an answer. "I would be the last person to ask," came the voice, which was how he met Elisabeth von Schalla. "I like a tune, almost any tune," Delage went on. "It's not a lot to ask. Do you think our pianist knows what his fingers are up to? Or is it the contraption he's trying to play? That's an old piano making heavy weather of it, I feel like blocking my ears." She was younger than he was, ten years, a rough guess, which would explain why she listened to him, instead of getting up and changing seats. He persevered. "I am not 110 percent sure he's a professional pianist anyway. Where did he get the tan? A pianist usually spends all his time indoors. He looks more like a ski-instructor, playing a bit of piano on the side. Knitted gloves. He would have learned to play by blowing into his hands and wearing knitted gloves. You probably don't know, but where I come from there's a hell of a lot of snow." He felt he had to say something. "Every year in our winter, plane-loads of Swiss and Austrian ski-instructors fly in, and work the ski resorts, taking our women." Again Delage wondered what he was doing in such a large room in Vienna, the strange impenetrable aspects of it. He could hear himself talking too much, as if he was talking to himself—one way of showing exasperation. And while he went on talking his eyes rested on Amalia von Schalla's head and shoulders there in the front row, the refined gray-blond hair pulled together with an oval-shaped diamond clasp which seemed to flash signals back at him. To think that he had come to Europe with one and only one aim, to introduce to the world his new piano, a truly remarkable design, "if I do say so myself," only to find his attention and therefore crucial energies drawn to the Austrian woman, a woman from the upper echelons, that was for sure, who had the softness to show some interest in him. Sun from the porthole divided her body at an angle. "My mother said you did not know anybody there, apart from her," Elisabeth said in a vague sort of voice. She sat up, proud of her breasts. "Aren't you pleased I went looking for you?" The music had stopped, the man in the bulging black T-shirt stepped forward without introduction, both he and his opinions being well known in Vienna, at least to the so-called intelligentsia, the cognoscenti, without notes, the much-feared music critic of the daily newspaper, squinted and began speaking in rasping German. “What’s he on about? I don’t understand a word he’s saying.” Leaning against him, she breathed into his ear as she translated. “To say that Austria is the land of neurosis is to say something we do not need to hear any more. It is what the English call ‘old hat.’ In the same basket I put the figure of the mediocre watercolorist, undoubtedly one of our most successful exports, the devotee of *Tristan*, who took his impotence and his many rejections and disappointments out on the world, and I won’t bother to mention, as a by-the-way, his sympathizers, still alive, prominent citizens, and doing well in Vienna . . .” The speaker took a few steps backward and forward. “There is a different malaise now, just as insidious. Europe is tired. This city we call Vienna is tired. A spiritual and artistic exhaustion is here. Vienna is a broad face with half-closed eyes, stone circles under the eyes. And the eyes are old man’s eyes. It has always been difficult producing something exceptional. It is more difficult now. Hemmed in on all sides our writers are crazed, become vitriolic, repetitious, misanthropic, anti-state, catch alight. We all have our heroes who have committed suicide. Here every artistic endeavor shifts forward, then gets caught up in the circles.” From the front row Berthe Clothilde turned to her audience, smiling for their approval. It is always interesting to hear somebody attack their place of birth, the interpreter could have been smiling as she kept her mouth close to Delage’s ear. “The future is in other places. There are questions you should be asking. You are a pampered, complacent, self-satisfied, half-asleep lot who don’t care—see the way you sit smiling at me! You are satisfied with what you know, and nothing more. You think that is enough. It is not. It is not enough. All it means is you are not sufficiently new. You are facing the other direction. Isn't it time to look and listen beyond where you are? Wearing jewelry and silk neckties are in themselves not enough. You dress up and attend concerts, and the opera of course, always the opera, but you no longer listen. You are into repeats. Take up embroidery instead." This was more or less what Frank Delage had been saying for years to anyone who would listen, be open to the new, although the Austrian expressed it better, much better. Under the flattering light of the chandelier, the overweight unshaven critic, who had done nothing in his life but listen to music, or read sheet music, or books analyzing music and the lives and correspondence of the great composers, cut a shabby figure in black, waving his arms about. To Delage, the speaker had every right to be impatient—he was surrounded by the problem! At least Delage could show a way forward with his breakaway piano. "Without renewal," the mouth sighed into his ear, "everything falls in a heap, stays the same, doesn't move. Is that really what you want? New movements must be allowed, and there are improvements to old instruments—they are waiting for us all." At this point, the volunteer-translator began nibbling Delage's ear and, unable to do two things at once, she stopped whispering the words, they'd hardly spoken, they hadn't actually met, he didn't know who she was or what she wanted, let alone, had anybody asked, what she looked like. She had taken the seat next to him. With his eyes fixed on the fearless critic, he could feel her mouth smiling at his confusion, which suggested she was young, perhaps too young, but he couldn't turn just then to see. If he turned she'd be forced to stop, which would surely embarrass her, and he didn't want that; on the other hand, without translation he couldn't understand a word being said, aside from the occasional name, Schoenberg and Glenn Gould he recognized, music was something he didn't know a lot about, not in the fine details, he was a manufacturer, it happened to be concert grands, a narrow field, although it is amazing how businessmen are self-assured in other, entirely different fields, a businessman will have firm opinions on abstract art, or Russian history, or landscape gardening. The speaker was coming to the end, for all Delage knew, summing up by the look, it was hard to tell, he was moving his arms slowly, horizontally, like von Karajan requiring softness from the horns. In fact, as the restlessness of the audience showed, the speaker had shifted to questions of a philosophical nature, which would not normally interest Delage, who now concentrated on what was being said, while trying to work out the right response to the nibbling of his ear, an incident so unexpected it had become pleasant. "Music and the playing of music is important. Music does no harm, it is said. It's something conductors like to trot out when interviewed. I'm not sure about it. What is harm? Let us examine 'harm'—in a musical context—for a moment." The speaker knew his subject from every possible angle, he thought about little else, listened with his eyes closed, he hardly had time to shave or wash, it gave him an untidy concentrated authority, enough to attract a biggish crowd, although Delage noticed some of the men were nodding off or checking their watches. In Vienna, he was the man to talk to, no doubt about it, Delage decided, he'd introduce himself as soon as his lecture finished, if he could get near him. Perhaps he would write an article about the Delage piano for one of the newspapers, that alone would make the trip all the way from Australia worthwhile. To ready himself, he turned to the woman beside him, breaking the contact with his ear. She remained half facing him and didn't smile, while he thought perhaps he should smile, just a bit, to ease himself away, not wanting to show disapproval. She had a factual expression, as if nothing out of the ordinary had happened, slightly long face and blouse buttoned up to her throat, which didn't look chaste, if anything the opposite. In a foreign city, Delage was having more trouble than usual reading the signs, he resorted to an affected casualness, according to his sister in Brisbane, a nuisance to the rest of the world, she said, to women most of all. "Our hostess, Frau Clothilde—" She immediately nodded, "Her mother was one of Sigmund Freud's patients, before the war that is." "Really?" Delage was not sure what to say next. Elisabeth turned, "I don't think she looks hysterical either. A perfectly well-adjusted woman." Delage was watching the Bertolt Brecht lookalike who had stopped in mid-sentence, a tall man with an anxious look had hurried in from the side and taken his elbow to tell him, Delage learned later, his house near Ottakring had caught fire and was still ablaze; without another word, the critic hurriedly left. "He's going, and I was keen to see him. I had something I wanted to talk about." Again, Delage felt to one side of whatever was happening, an opportunity was there but moved away from him. Elisabeth stood up. "I'm looking for my mother. I'm coming right back."

Delage never went into Athens to see for himself how the most learned, graceful and philosophical city had become the ugliest, crassest, most disgraceful of cities, all sense of proportion trashed, along with imparted wisdom; what a people to allow it. At least Port Said, a few days later, where he had a haircut on the footpath while the ship unloaded European textbooks, electronics, medical instruments to take on Egyptian brass lamps, dates, cotton tea towels, there were no disappointments, it was all matter-of-fact, wide open in the brown heat, a straightforward mess with no reminders of previous grandeur, figures lay asleep on benches, the eucalyptus tree, dreamy slow-motion movement, the figures in long costume or else wearing cheap shirts, all of which left him in a stationary position, a person in a false situation, he distinctly felt. "Do you think there's a piano here—anywhere? I don't think so." In hot countries, the weather favors drums and single-string instruments, and their repetitious melancholy, a grand piano would require tuning every other day. They were in a park, Elisabeth seated beside him. The other passengers went off in different directions, their alertness to novel sights gave the impression they had more energy than the locals, an optical illusion, most likely. Delage was happy to remain seated in the park with Elisabeth, a small crowd of men stood around watching. It was one thing to sit down at meals with virtual strangers and make polite conversation, quite another to step off the ship and join them sightseeing. There is always a leader who attracts the timid, the conventional, it is how the European political and piano world has operated for centuries, to its detriment, Delage was looking down at his shoes and up at the young men looking at him, the majority fall into line behind the most established name in pianos, the least progressive piano, too afraid to take another path, as it is in all aspects of the world. "There I was, I experienced it firsthand. And I'm not impressed," he said to her. The two weeks spent in Vienna had passed quickly. Elisabeth's father told Delage from behind his ornate desk that his life up to sixty-five had passed slowly, but now approaching old age it began passing quickly. "Something for you to look forward to, perhaps," with the faintest smile. Seated in the shade on a stone bench (so this is Port Said?), hemmed in by flat-roofed concrete buildings, people nearby slow-moving, watchful, he felt the opportunities for his Australian-made piano dissolving as Europe receded. There was no sign of Europe from where he was sitting. From the downtrodden park in Egypt, it didn't exist, he could have been somewhere in outer space, Elisabeth seated beside him, providing a noticeable presence of loyalty, that was something; already he had difficulty remembering Vienna and its traffic, its heavy circles of architecture. It goes without saying they would stick their noses up in the air at an intruder, a concert grand made in a hopeless backward place, Australia. "Probably the wrong thing to do, going to Vienna. It had to be done, but I went too early—I'd say by about two years," he was saying, more or less to himself. “An expensive mistake, a fiasco, it achieved absolutely bloody nothing.” And never had he talked so much as he had in Vienna. “A fiasco did you say?” “That’s right.” In Sydney he would go for long periods without talking, or talking as little as possible, months would pass, then without any reason he’d begin talking his head off, something triggered it, whatever, there was nothing stopping him, whether talking to a single person or an entire table, they would hang on his every word, so it seemed to him, holding forth on a subject, packing it with information, not only about his piano, plenty of other subjects too, his line of thought wandering as he introduced other thoughts, other angles, so many possibilities and facts out there, including complaints, before bringing it back to the original subject, he could be amazing, very persuasive. This was Frank Delage. Sometimes even he had to remind himself. And his sister used to complain he didn’t talk enough, that is, to her, but as he grew older he knew he was talking more, coming out with pointless sayings and recollections and suggestions that went on too long, just as his street directions went on and on, there are women after a certain age who talk too much, cannot stop themselves, going on without pause, a word-flow not allowing an entry point, it was a habit he wouldn’t want to become established, he didn’t want to go down that path. “At least one thing of interest came out of Vienna, wouldn’t you say?” still with her head turned. Delage laughed. Here he was on a stone bench in Egypt with the archetypal blond from upper Austria, except she was unusual, very, her visual characteristic was indifference. “My sister I've told you about keeps telling me I exaggerate. She of course is someone who's never exaggerated in her entire life." "I have not noticed exaggeration." But Elisabeth showed little interest in what he was doing, or was trying to do with his piano. If anything, she shrugged at the subject and at the broad polished object itself, as if she wanted to avoid anything to do with music, while Delage talked too much about it. At least he had plenty of other things to say—when they occurred to him. "Why are we being stared at by these boys? Do they not have something better to do?" Even this she said in a languid way, as if she was accustomed to hot countries, such as Saudi Arabia nearby, or Laos, Cambodia, Burma, countries that were humid as well as hot, whereas the only hot countries she had been to were Spain and northern Italy, when she was a student. "It's not me they're interested in," he said. "They only have eyes for you. If I were them I'd be doing the same." Delage had been addressing a postcard to his sister, and stood up. There were five other passengers on the *Romance*, Dutch, English, two sisters from Melbourne, in each case their hair, skin, firmness of jaw, parts of clothing made them recognizable from specific parts of the world. The Dutchman introduced himself as Zoellner (bookseller, Amsterdam); to Elisabeth, the sisters were "very sure of their place, very. I cannot understand why." One followed the other in divorce or separation, it doesn't matter which, now sister-companions, six years apart. The Englishman, from Folkestone, was a blinker, always at short intervals an eruption of blinking, tiring to watch—wife equally tall, alongside. The cabins were a surprise, decked out in brown carpet. Delage's had a desk, an office chair. It was supposed to be the second engineer's cabin, it said on the door, but it had been many years since a second engineer was needed on such container ships. Above the bed a large porthole faced the containers stacked in their different colors to the bow, the yellow gantry almost touched the window as it came forward, loading or unloading the "boxes," so they are called. Elisabeth's cabin was directly below. Most of the time she spent with Delage, and yet she didn't seem to want anything. She slept in his bed.

But at last the sun was free of clouds, she wanted to go out on deck, nothing else mattered, such a smooth pale body, she allowed him to watch, although he was thinking about something else; she stepped aside for him to work the lever to open the hatch, the decks were on either side of the great funnel, barely enough room on these decks (brick-red painted floors) to swing a cat. "The watery part of the world," Delage had written down. The sun glittered on the last of the Mediterranean and lit up other ships, the breadth of the sea even here rendering them toylike, as if in a metal tub, or a series of shuttles in slow motion passing across a silvery loom. As Elisabeth talked she turned her back to the scene, Delage reduced his answers to nodding, striving to know her, until he hardly talked at all. "My mother never puts water on her face," she said, apropos of nothing in particular, "only rose water."

The main body of seated guests broke into separate bodies, Delage to one side. No one could recall a speaker at one of Berthe's soirées bolting from the room in mid-sentence, without a word of explanation, let alone apology, even if he was a critic and therefore ridiculously over-confident, it goes with the job or the mentality, he could be excused perhaps, an illness in the family, a death or a very serious car accident, it had to be something in that area, not even an opinionated critic could be so thoughtless. No one in her circle knew the tragedy that had befallen the speaker, Berthe had no information, she enjoyed being asked, her lack of information added to the mystery, which in turn could only bolster the already high reputation of her every-third-Friday gatherings, the most well-attended in Vienna, not that she had any rivals as active, where the lucky visitor was bound to encounter fresh knowledge, the poetic unexpected. Instead, she went from group to group demanding their opinions on what the music critic said, before he had dropped his bundle and left, in the nicest way possible she expressed disappointment in the men who clearly hadn't been listening, which made her turn abruptly to their wives, it was the presence and the words of men she preferred. Berthe Clothilde tended to latch on to men with an unhealthy, undivided attention. Everybody knew her mother had been one of Freud's last patients in Vienna; they were neighbors on Berggasse. According to Berthe, who presented an unnatural calm, the treatment had made her mother worse—without going into details. In some cases, talking about hysteria, and possibly even revealing the sources of it, apparently can make a person even more hysterical. The weekly sessions with Freud were something her mother looked forward to, Berthe Clothilde told Elisabeth, her mother felt it like a death when he left Vienna. The treatment made her worse, but she was even worse after he left. The massive chandelier, the Steinway grand, the porcelain plates and vases, the blue-and-gold swirling wallpaper, the men and women conversing in twos and threes, some already smoking cigarettes, kept Delage to one side, waiting for Elisabeth to return, while trying to catch a glimpse of her mother who had abandoned him. Amalia von Schalla and her daughter were the only people he knew in Vienna, the mother he knew more than the daughter, yet it could hardly be said he knew her at all. It had always been women who had shown him kindness and sympathy, something he found hard to reciprocate. "It's beyond my capacity," a wood-carver at the factory had once said about a new way to curve timber. Here under the ostentatiously large chandelier it was a matter of adopting a patient, unconscious stance, which came easily to Delage, and could possibly attract a person or two, unlikely, but you never know, out of pity or curiosity, or because they too felt isolated, someone on the fringe might break away and introduce themselves, a common occurrence at cocktail parties, one of their few attractions. But although the speaker had been unshaven and wore a grubby T-shirt, the audience under the chandelier appeared stiff in dress and movement. They too were comfortable in what they had chosen. Even Delage could see the quality of their suits and ties, women wearing trim jackets, hair done for the occasion, jewelry. Of course he could take the initiative and select an unsuspecting person who was also ignored by the majority, and begin by giving his impressions of Vienna and the Austrian people, if they were interested, before switching to the Delage piano and its advantages—after all, that was the reason he was standing there in a stately room in Vienna. It had been Amalia who arranged the invitation to Berthe's soirée. And Berthe didn't allow just anybody in. Some people had been waiting years to get in, and would continue to wait, pulling every string they could think of, evidently the wrong sort of strings, for there was little chance these people would ever be allowed in. Now instead of mixing with the upper echelons of Vienna's musical world, many of them in this one room, although he couldn't recognize any of them, Delage remained to one side, thinking about all kinds of things other than pianos and concert performances, Sydney streets and glittering water, for example, the factory floor (its cleanliness), which he always liked, close-up of accountant's pouting mouth, at the same time trying to slow down his thinking or, far more difficult, stop thinking altogether. If he succeeded it was not by managing to be empty of all thoughts, more that he couldn't recall what they were, especially when Elisabeth broke in—"What are you thinking?" Having to think what he had just been thinking about was not the same as thinking. Delage's tendency was to stand back and not say a word, before rushing in with his own considered thoughts, his own positions, whether people liked it or not, enough to deflect or derail, at least it announced his thinking, producing mixed results. His thoughts kept returning to Amalia von Schalla, how he had touched her, which she had allowed. And there she was down the front, so he looked on, and waited. If the chandelier had loosened and fallen, bringing down the ceiling with it, onto the heads of the smartly dressed people, whose refuge from ordinariness was in taste, sensibility, an irreplaceable section of Austrian society would have been wiped out, or at least severely injured and covered in dust, reminiscent of the last hours in Hitler's bunker. He could see Elisabeth still talking to her mother. "Are you dining with the Schallas?"—Berthe Clothilde at his elbow. Already she was waving goodbye to an unusually short couple, the woman wearing a green felt hat. "One of our composers. You wouldn't know who he is." Delage felt Elisabeth's hand on his arm. "I am to look after you. You are not to be out of my sight." While nodding he looked over to where her mother had been standing but she was no longer there. "You can call me Elisabeth, if you want." She said she hadn't eaten all day. As they left the Clothilde house he wondered whether he had offended her mother, Amalia, women don't usually turn their backs without a reason, they're always making a point of some sort. His hand had reached out and touched, as if it had a life of its own, obeying an affinity was how it felt. To think about it made him smile. Elisabeth was different, modest, yet unconventional, she had a freshness, easy to be with; she gave herself. From the beginning, Delage saw traces of her mother, even if it was out of the corner of his eye, the shape of her nose relocated, losing a little precision along the way, their shared neatness of hair, skin, dress. He didn't know what he was expected to do. Out on the street, Elisabeth revealed more of her mother's straight back, she could have stepped off a show-jumper, but was not as tall as her mother, he saw at once. "It looks like rain," Delage was about to say, or better still, “It rains more in Vienna than Sydney,” but instead he opened and twisted his mouth, as if it was filled with water. Aside from drawing attention to the obvious (it had begun raining) it would only give the impression he was in awkward anticipation of the next few minutes. More and more he realized he stated the obvious in order to assist the other person, it’s better to say very little, or indicate a certain amount of reserve, which at least had the merit of not appearing hasty, and suggested a degree of wisdom, taking her arm crossing the street, she was at least ten years younger—which gave her the advantage. Often Delage was unsure of what expression to have on his face, especially when alone on a street or standing around waiting for somebody; not long ago his sister had caught him pulling faces in her kitchen, when he made the mistake of visiting her in Ashgrove, Brisbane, she said it showed he hadn’t grown up. Only a man who isn’t comfortable with himself pulled silly faces, as she put it, not stopping there as she rattled the pots and pans, most men she knew were infantile, they suffered from “infantile paralysis,” which was a nuisance, she added with a firmness Delage found irritating. She was prone to exaggerations. There was no reason behind most of the things she said. As far as he knew, she had little or no experience of men, it was a wonder she’d ever sat alone in a room with one. At least he had been married, “Victoria”—an initial starburst, it didn’t last. It became uneven, he could feel it loosening, a marriage with holes in it, so many he didn’t quite know where the marriage itself was, still it went on, two people together but turning away, when the design of the new piano was at its most intractable, as intractable as the problems of his marriage, which made it easier, he told himself, not to be there. Living alone had not been his sister's choice, Delage could see, she swung her exaggerations around to him, her brother who managed to live in another city. Each morning Delage woke and enjoyed a sense of well-being, there was clarity, the whole day spread out before him. Delage didn't mind living alone, it was something he never thought about, now here he was on a ship in a carpeted cabin with Elisabeth von Schalla, a woman at least ten years younger; she had more or less moved in without asking. "I've decided to take less interest in concert grands. I'm sick of them. I'm going to focus all my tremendous energies on people, beginning with people I already know," he told Elisabeth, although he could have been talking to the sky. "What do you say? Forget it, I'm just thinking aloud." Of course he wasn't about to finish with the Delage piano, what with all its inventions (patents pend.), the various refinements, just because he'd come up against a few difficulties in Vienna. "You may have left it too late," was her reply. Having crossed the street he wanted to know where they were going. It was here on Karolinengasse, she stopped in front of the building, where a piano being lifted through a window slipped out of its sling, cartwheeled five stories onto the footpath "this far from me," she bent her arm at the elbow, aged seventeen, a student, the piano's lid smashing into the windscreen of a parked car. She leaned against him, "I was only seventeen. I could have been killed." "What we call a close shave," Delage looking up at the window. A close call. "There's more metal than people think in a piano. You'd end up being this high. You would have been splattered all over the place. Blood everywhere. Bones sticking out in all directions. Did it leave a hole in the footpath—or even a dent? They can cause a serious injury too." Elisabeth had stopped walking. "I don't think you are treating me seriously." Exaggeration had brought them closer, although he was determined not to smile. And Elisabeth too had exaggerated, for the recollection was never going to equal the crashing force of the event, nor the sensation of escape, standing there now at the very spot, her pale fine skin, aware of her soft blood which was living warmth. The sight of a piano being destroyed imposes silence on the bystander. There was that concert grand, a Bechstein, by the look, which had been converted into a coffin, with hundreds of small faces painted inside the lid, some sort of war protest, he told Elisabeth, who knew all about it. "Performance Art," she gave a little sigh, Basel in the early '70s, Delage had seen photographs and almost had one doctored for the company Christmas card, before thinking better of it. Pianos lie in silence at the bottom of the ocean; those destroyed in European cities, collapsing under the bricks of burning buildings, others left exposed in a room above the street, wallpaper flapping, in German cities in particular, home of music, Poland, Hungary too, of course, thousands of perfectly good pianos were lost to the world then. Many were used in barricades, a piano left smoldering—talk about an image of old Europe. As they advance into houses, it is known that soldiers destroy musical instruments, there is an impulse to destroy signs of the previous serene life, not as senseless as it may seem, pianos machine-gunned, violins smashed against walls. Vienna had a brooding quality, something still going on. Delage wondered whether he should return to his hotel, simplicity beckoned, an early night, just him, himself in his room, he hadn't stopped since he had landed in Vienna, each movement was a blow to his habits. "After your narrow escape, I suppose you run the other way at the sight of a piano." He felt too tired to be sufficiently alert. "My mother told me you are clever." It wasn't how Delage saw himself. People impressed with one quality of a person use it to describe their other qualities. "We are inviting you to eat with us. My mother entrusted me. You may have other arrangements, something more interesting. Do you know our nightclubs? They are the best in the world." Without answering, he kept walking with Elisabeth, who took his arm. Back in his hotel room he would have sat with his hands on his knees and contemplated his future, he was here on business, after all, he had to get on with it, to establish some sort of foothold, or "beach head," as he almost shouted at them back at the factory. One way forward would be to enlist the support of the music critic, if he could find a way of meeting him. If Vienna remained indifferent, he could always turn to Berlin. Instead he was heading toward Amalia von Schalla, handsome unsmiling woman, a regal presence, until he had reduced the gap with his hand, he lingered more on her, the mother, than her fast-forward daughter, he knew virtually nothing about her, even less about the daughter, Elisabeth, now striding with purpose. The best of his intentions were being derailed by a determination or an interest he could not understand, not fully, everything he was seeing was unusual, he may have appeared as a novelty to them, mother and daughter, certainly there were things all around him he was not accustomed to, in a strange dark city where the surrounding language was foreign, he became all too aware of his limitations, take away the piano and he represented nothing, or very little. At the same time he wanted to expand beyond the mechanics of the piano. More and more he saw himself as someone without edges, the imprecision, one who easily became indifferent, after a certain distance he tended to fade. It happened to people close by, those coming closer, turning them away. When he looked around he saw this wasn't unusual. He had been getting nowhere in Vienna. If he took up the invitation to dinner he might pick up some useful contacts or tips, the whereabouts of the music critic, for example. "Was it your mother's idea, or yours?" "Does it matter?"—the answer he expected, pointed to her. Now they were heading toward her, Amalia von Schalla, standing in a room above a street somewhere, he imagined, not at all fitting the usual idea of the mother, just because she had a daughter, even in the way he imagined her waiting with arms folded. As the rain stopped, Delage noticed Elisabeth was a woman who sighed, so someone else had a habit entrenched, gave little sighs for no reason, the way some people crack their knuckles, or clunk their teeth with a spoon when they eat, in her mid-thirties and a gentle habit had been allowed to form, she may no longer be aware of it, only child, Delage sighed, the sighs were almost imperceptible, now and then a deeper, louder sigh, all of which had nothing to do with disappointment, exhaustion, unhappiness, Elisabeth was free of such troubles. "Always sighing is no help," written down. When he heard another sigh, Delage found himself smiling, her breast moved against his arm, he listened for her sighs, before wondering whether anyone spending time with Elisabeth would become irritated by them.

She wasn't interested in the ship tied with lines against the wharf, it was hard to know what Elisabeth was interested in, immaculate, waiting patiently while Delage stood admiring the bulging mass of orange-painted steel, it reared out of the green water, colossal in volume, its height and length went on forever, without snapping in two. To Frank Delage, it was a marvel of welded engineering; impossible surely for anybody not to be impressed, except, that is, Elisabeth. Fat in the water, it leaked streams of water, as well as small sounds, creaking and groaning metal, humming, and slowly hissed steam, wisps of smoke coming out of somewhere; all this the piano manufacturer from Sydney found interesting. As soon as he made an observation to Elisabeth, he could hear a pedantic tone coming from his mouth and nose, better to try out exaggerated explanations. At intervals the ship let out sighs, sometimes he confused them with the sighs Elisabeth gave out, alongside him. In the beginning he had wondered whether Elisabeth's habit came from boredom, or else tiredness, she could have been tired, lack of oxygen to the lungs; unhappiness with a mother or father, of life in general, is known to bring on sighing. Women throw themselves into various tasks with tremendous energy, then collapse in a heap, suddenly tired: "the wreck of the Hesperus" he had heard only women say, his mother and close behind, his sister, women in the office too, the one time they don't mind appearing gaunt. Telling Elisabeth ordinary things made her laugh, sometimes the English words didn't fit, she had to listen carefully, it was one of the things he liked. To go ashore they took small steps down a steep gangplank, which had a rope for a railing, Elisabeth in glossy high heels, to reach the street, which had an oil-stained scrappy surface, they had to run between whirring forklifts carrying containers, warning lights flashing, men shouting, pausing for the tall grubby yellow gantry coming toward them along rails parallel to the ship. In her home city, Vienna, he had allowed Elisabeth to lead him about, here she turned to him for knowledge of the ship, the docks, the dangers, his second or third experience of the activities of docks. "See how she looked at me? I don't think that woman likes me." Delage hadn't noticed, not necessarily disagreeing, said, "Don't you find when sisters are together it's difficult? They each influence the other." The passengers kept walking up and down the street alongside the docks, stepping around the potholes, at the same time not letting the ship out of their sight, trailed by boys offering postcards, cigarettes, bottles of water, bananas. We can go further afield, Delage decided. The further they went from the ship the less he thought about the piano standing on its legs back in Vienna, and the different disturbances it had produced across the city which had affected people's lives in a "ripple effect," he was with the woman from Vienna who had left Vienna to be nearby, he wondered what she could see in him, the way she came on board with that smile and significantly heavy suitcases, without knowing the near future, or the distant future, let alone the merits or otherwise of a city like Sydney, if he had asked about her plans he would have become cornered, he thought; he allowed his thoughts to wander without purpose from the colossal orange ship to the pale shape of her, to the streets, palm trees that needed water, dirt, always a few single men looking on, when what he wanted was clarity, not entirely but when necessary. Some children running ahead bumped into the group, the bookseller actually tipped his hat, old school, the two sister-companions from Elwood, Melbourne, fanning themselves with colored magazines, Delage's thoughts had already slowed to a standstill, the English couple in the lead, tall timber, the older of the short-haired sister-companions looking Elisabeth up and down whenever she could, not a happy woman, no wonder she had been discarded, it was the other one who did the talking. "Watch the handbag, it'll get pinched." Only a few hours before, they'd been on the ship at the one table having breakfast, now as a way to move on Delage made light of the moment, in a loud voice: "Can you recommend any monuments?" "The pyramids, I believe, are that-a-way," the Englishman joining in. He wore a royal-blue knitted cotton shirt with buttons, and a gold watch. "That man," Delage told Elisabeth, "has a real-estate agency in the south of England somewhere, and knows all there is to know about Gothic churches. He's a walking Oxford dictionary on the subject. And he does his best to hide what he knows. I don't mind him at all." An Englishman who responded modestly and honestly to the solidarity of things, taking one step at a time, waiting before crossing the village street, a sequence which had produced strength in British engineering, medicine, law, science, the cataloguing of libraries, the design of umbrellas, as well as a pedantic tone in its literature, and art unable to shake an unhealthy obsession with the naked figure. They had been on the ship a week or so, Delage found himself glancing at her, Elisabeth, still not knowing enough about her, that was why, until he began being direct by looking direct; if she noticed, she would turn slightly, out of politeness or believing it showed her best side. The Dutchman had joined in and told them he regularly attended literary evenings, standing on one leg for hours at a time, drinking sour wine, while poets read aloud from their works, until it had ruined his health, not only his physical health, the Dutchman emphasized, had a large face and large eyes, but his psychological health as well, which was worse, he said, far worse, the result of taking in an exceptional amount of the most earnest, pointless words, very damaging, just as the body cannot be exposed to excessive X-rays, words and still more words of little or no value, even by well-known poets, who often had the worst reading voices, just as the worst poets had the best reading voices. "The poorest countries have the biggest postage stamps," Delage chimed in. It was not only poets, the Dutchman went on, novelists and even, believe it or not, historians, biographers and journalists jump at the chance to give public readings, anything to be on stage and listened to by a live audience. It was the age of performance. Why anybody would go to the trouble of putting on a fresh pair of trousers, go out into the weather, take the tram or bus, find the venue, and hand across hard-earned money, in order to listen to an author was, he could see now, beyond his comprehension. "Years of my life have been wasted combing my hair, and attending festivals, and listening to writers reading. The years wasted. And there's nothing I can do about it now, which only makes it worse. I lie wide awake at night." The two sisters had nothing against poetry readings, one of them had written poems herself. At literary festivals, which have spread like an infectious disease across the western world, a by-product of prosperity, the connection just came to him, the Dutchman, there is a never-ending stream of opinions spoken by writers, either they're reading aloud or else seated on stage discussing their books, or tackling other weighty subjects such as free-market economics, or Islam and censorship, or whether it's possible to write a good poem with a baby at your feet, or death, subjects they have little or no knowledge of, but still they keep on talking instead of writing, and are listened to reverently. The Dutchman had become exasperated at what he saw around him, "trash and camera-vanity," one producing the other, "there is nothing firm underneath," as he put it, his wife complained he never had anything positive to say, she enjoyed literary festivals, and after twenty-three years of marriage had left him, "an otherwise ordinary Saturday, taking just a suitcase, and wearing a raincoat," and moved in with some women who were obsessed with puppet theater. "I am hoping the sea voyage will settle my nerves," he said. The audience was small on the ship. People require distraction as never before, the Dutchman told them. What to do in our leisure time is the most important question today. It hasn't been answered yet. "They could think about playing a piano," Delage said to Elisabeth. "Opening night at galleries is the worst," she said. "I don't ever want to go to another one. You and I met at a lecture, but it could hardly be called public. It was someone lecturing about music, wasn't it? I wasn't paying much attention." The strangeness of Port Said was strange in an ordinary way, small traders, large trucks, many gaps, and they felt slow and strange toward one another, wandering into side streets at random, the further they went from the ship the more they found the town and each other interesting. They were polite to each other, almost too careful, Frank Delage thinking it necessary to make a firm impression, while avoiding the false step. Figures lay asleep on concrete benches, "concrete," he decided to tell Elisabeth, "because of termites." "Termites?" checking on his seriousness, "How do you know that?" Further on she asked, "What is it you would like to know about me?" How many other men had she slept with? was one question that came to mind, a distant curiosity, little more, which he would never get around to asking. Instead it was her mother, remote yet attentive, who invited questions and slid away, replaced by her daughter, now by his side, who had parts of the same smooth face, Amalia von Schalla's, the same way too of extending a silence, all of which interested him. Past the mosque, what could have been a mosque, a side-street mosque, the boy in a white shirt, followed by another, threw a stone, others followed, one hitting Delage on the neck, he took Elisabeth by the elbow. "It would appear we're not wanted here. Better not rush it." The same boys brushed past, six or seven, different sizes. As they came in close, Delage reached for the hand of one of them, held it tight, clicked his biro and carefully drew a face with big teeth and ears, the boy looked up at him, then waved his palm with a cry, the others came forward wanting theirs. They had passed the opera house. Delage was in her hands. It stopped raining, which was a precise moment he always liked. The many different kinds of gray, of black, patches of gray-black reflected, laid out on and at angles to the streets, rectangles of it tilted and glistened, glass had turned as dark as mirrors, mixed with what was rounded. Taking his hand, Elisabeth led him into the von Schalla apartments, walked in, and opened the door to the main room. "Mister Sydney Piano has agreed to join us." A silver-haired man in a dark suit reading a newspaper stood up. Elisabeth led Delage across a large apricot-colored carpet. Some people stand up and go forward, others remain standing and the visitor is forced to go forward. Visitors to Konrad von Schalla invariably wanted something, it was only to be expected he would remain in the one spot and for them to step forward, if it were the other way around, even meeting half-way, the advantage could shift at that moment from him to them, it didn't take much for the pendulum to shift, over the years hundreds of people in business and governments had arrived at the von Schalla apartments with requests, or offers, or suggestions, or whispers of some sort, information of course can be valuable, von Schalla standing up from his armchair or behind his tiny desk, so many people had crossed the large soft carpet, cap in hand, while he remained standing in the one spot, it had become a habit for him not to take a few steps forward, even to his own daughter. She kissed him and stepped back. "This is Mr. Delage from Sydney. He is the maker of a special piano. I think that is the way to describe you." Delage nodded at the small man who was looking at him. "Relax, I'm not here to sell you any grand pianos. I've just about given up on that. It's been hard to get a response. I met Mrs. Schalla yesterday. Beg your pardon, or was it the day before?" Amalia von Schalla had shown sympathy, and he had reached out and touched her breast. Delage didn't care what he said to this man, who remained looking at him, although he saw in the eyes a watery blue warning, what appeared to be a faint smile of welcome, or condescension, nodding rather than saying anything, taking his time, Delage glancing past his shoulder expecting, or at least preferring, to see Amalia. "You might tell your mother her guest has arrived," von Schalla said in German.

Wherever he looked there was another wave of different shape, different size, lengths of dissolving foam drawing the eye, the pink sofa obscenely dented with buttons he couldn't avoid, striped maroon armchairs by the fireplace, where Konrad von Schalla had risen from reading a newspaper, ebony-and-gold encrusted side tables, large lamps on tables, gold carvings and inlay erupting up and down legs, three clocks, two chandeliers, tall bulging vases, fireplace, the accumulating conflict of shapes and colors, the large yellowish carpet occupying the center like a pool infested with weed, bordered by a pattern, possibly flowers, the largest carpet Delage had ever seen. Ancestral portraits were on the wall, "looking down," military types favoring the large wave-breaking mustache. A few small landscapes, dark oils. "Do you find, in your line of business, Vienna is bogged down in the old ways?" Delage had pointed to the Steinway in the corner, which reminded him of his own difficulties. "Reputed to be Mahler's personal piano," von Schalla answered, perfect English, "but can you fully trust what people say?" Does a person mean what they say, even when it's based on a fact? Very often words are chosen to fit an expression (thoughtful, skeptical, surprised). "My wife can tell you all about its history. If interested, you could ask her." And it was too early to take up his next offer, "Sit down and play it, if you wish." In Europe it seemed people Delage encountered were in a hurry, each one acting as a concierge in a vast hotel, moving on to someone else, from one problem or opportunity to the next, and a certain sardonic manner had established itself, skepticism as a way to live, at the very least. There was no sign of Amalia, her daughter had disappeared too. In their conversations often they went back to the night he had first met her father, and his impressions, the enormous drawing room, where his eyes couldn't rest, the way her mother made an entrance, in a contrasting simplicity of dark gray dress. Now it was Elisabeth's turn to show indifference. She appeared dressed for dinner while Delage was talking to her mother, who had a gaunt attentiveness, she was graying, the fine lines around her mouth too, Delage saw, which produced in him a wave of intimate respect, once a beauty, now handsome, a raised-chin beauty, Elisabeth her daughter passed before them, similar shoulders, to sit in the striped armchair where she angled her legs to the floor, high heels, these were Spanish designer shoes, a butterfly embroidered on her stocking. "You're frowning—at what?" Amalia von Schalla asked. Delage had averted his eyes from the daughter, in her mid-thirties she had an inappropriate ribbon in her hair, her reckless neckline which encouraged him to put imaginary hands down and onto them, take one or both in his hands, their warm pointed volume, making an estimate if nothing else, it was the same with most men, perhaps every one of them. And Frank Delage in Europe, one among the many millions on the streets, began to feel he could do or say anything; he was more free in the Schalla drawing room than in Sydney, where he was known. Elisabeth looked away, not recognizing her effect on him, Delage returning to Amalia, as she explained the government subsidy of Vienna's orchestras, although he was not interested, a paltry amount apparently, a fraction of what, for example, Konrad von Schalla, looking on, invested in his cement factories or chain of hotels every week. A neat man, he barely came up to Delage's shoulders. He wore a dark striped suit. The corners of the white handkerchief protruding from the lapel, the sails of the Sydney Opera House, perhaps that was where the architect Utzon found his inspiration, an overrated piece of architecture, if ever there was, a sacred building in Sydney, in all of Australia, based on a white handkerchief, in the glare of daylight it shouts out "over-emphasize," and therefore "provincial," anything to catch attention, softer, more complex, thoughtful at night, and the acoustics are terrible. So many things in the world are arranged for the eyes, not the mind. The Dutchman had one elbow on the rail, gazing at the passing waves, trails of dissolving foam, "We should not be disapproving of repetition. Each day we see the same things, eyes, noses and legs, the trees and clouds, and each day we repeat the same words. And we never stop doing the same things over and over again, every day, sleeping, cleaning our teeth, shaking hands, drinking tea, sitting on a chair, which give stability to our lives. It is necessary. Daily repetitions form part of what we call love, I can see now—it's been my mistake." Alone or with someone alongside Delage could happily spend hours following the waves, each one replacing another. The Dutchman went on as if he weren't there. "The repetitions we experience in ordinary life are so natural they ought to flow into literature, into novels most of all. The great Russians knew. It became their style. It is noticeable today when writers read aloud from their works, and something is missing. Repetitions are part of our existence. These waves—never stop. It is all very obvious. But repetitions are the first things publishers today want to strike out." Delage sat at the table in the small dining room, not the long table in the long dining room, where antlers of different sizes filled one wall, Elisabeth facing him, her mother to the left, he could admire her hands, von Schalla to his right, as the ponderous footman put the tip of his tongue out each time he poured the wine. The glasses had green spiral stems. "Do you have white wines in your country?" What a stupid bloody question. Delage raised his glass, "We have whites, but not much yellow like this." Elisabeth was still smiling, her mother not looking at anybody. "It comes from our vineyard at Wachau. I mean to say, it has been in my wife's family for generations. As have these glasses." The wines of Austria was a subject he would like to talk about, his wife and daughter had not the slightest interest, wines were the furthest things from their minds at any given time, but all Delage knew was that Austrian red wines were even worse than Californian, Chilean or South African. It was then that Amalia von Schalla, on Delage's left, said how interesting the evening at the Clothildes had been, at which her husband gave a snort. "Berthe's not as bad as that," his wife said. "In fact, what was being said was extremely interesting, and very apt, I thought, until the speaker had to leave in the midst of it." She turned to Delage, "I believe his house caught fire. Everything he owned was lost. Musical scores, program notes, his record collection, all his books on music. It was his entire world." "Who are you talking about?" von Schalla asked. Here Delage tried to help out, "A critic who got up and told everybody to their faces they were lazy and tradition-bound, a self-satisfied lot, letting modern music down. No surprises there, if my experience is anything to go by. What I found interesting was that it had no effect whatsoever. Everybody sat nodding, with their hands on their laps. And as he went on hurling abuse at them, he also said something about Austrian writers being egocentric, repetitious and vitriolic. I wouldn't know about that. The piano is my field.

And I was having it all translated for me." He winked at Elisabeth, as von Schalla began dabbing his mouth with a napkin, "And you say his house caught fire? What some people will do to attract attention." Delage thought Amalia had been left isolated, though it was difficult to know, she remained aloof. He said to her, "The fire, that sounds bad for him. Did you know him at all? He was someone I was keen to meet." A patch of sun from the deck crossed the side of his face, and remained, the white glare magnified the soft surface, brought the spots and silver hairs forward, small broken veins, a general life-tiredness, more than the Dutchman realized, still talking, oblivious to the light, which encouraged inspection, although forced to squint. He was careless about his appearance. He wasn't interested. Here and there Delage's body showed signs of wear, of his years, of ignoring his sister's dietary and exercise advice, even his hands continued as factory hands, none of this he thought about until now, Elisabeth's younger body, clean, smooth, gradual in its contours. They were leaving the Mediterranean, the other passengers had emerged to see, leaving Europe. Delage went down to get Elisabeth. After the coffee, Delage had touched Elisabeth on the shoulder as he followed her mother out of the room, to indicate "her suggestion," following her along the corridor, the long carpet called a "runner," it came to him, reddish-pink, it went on forever, tapestries, alabaster nymphs and other figurines, mirrors, entablature and what-not, to one of the doors toward the end, "cluttered houses, cluttered minds," she was saying. Amalia opened the door and switched on the light. It was a white room, unexpectedly sparse, just a few paintings, cubist and geometric abstract, one entirely black, and a bookshelf in two stages painted red and black. Two chrome-legged reclining chairs faced a low green sofa. Nothing in Delage's appearance gave a clue as to his profession, partly because only a handful of piano designer-manufacturers were left in the world, and nobody knew anymore what they looked like. These chairs were the kind chosen by architects the world over, just as architects the world over, and not only progressive ones, dress in the same black shirt, black jacket, almost-black trousers, the progressive architect's uniform, it follows they specify the same black leather chairs and sofas for their interiors, whether they're comfortable or not, everything in its place at the precise angle, altogether a statement by Amalia von Schalla on being clear, unencumbered, modern, in contrast to the rest of the von Schalla house, to Vienna itself, to her marriage. "These are my apartments. This is where I come and sit." He turned to her again—and what a laugh, her mouth open and wide, a laugh involving him. It was a matter of joining in, although he didn't know why, not quite, laughing away with her. He had hardly come across her kind of woman before, a remote beauty, if it was beauty, which now softened, the laugh had calmed down to a broad smile, enough to encourage his hand to her waist, where it remained, while looking at the near-empty room. "It suits you," he decided, "I think it does." He moved his hand to the back of her head. "Do you like it as a room?" If he had not gone to Europe to introduce his new piano, it would not be happening. "It's very much you. Of course, I like it." The over-decorated rest of the house and the over-decorated city outside must have been setting her teeth on edge. Her aesthetic principles were modern, there was progress in art, even in furnishings, perhaps it included pianos, advances in their original design, which was why he was in Vienna, stroking her hair. The modernity of the room encouraged movement, Amalia may have felt it that way, allowing him to draw her closer, in the same movement taking her breast, she was allowing the strange hand, Delage continued, although he was perplexed. She was difficult to know, but now a small part was released. He was on the verge of saying something, he thought he should, almost anything, when she gave an unexpected push, a slap stinging his cheek. Delage could go only a small way in understanding a person, beyond a certain point he could never know their thoughts, or their way of thinking, the surface of a person was only that. Unexpected behavior took him by surprise more than it should. The door had opened, von Schalla was standing there, small neat figure in the well-tailored suit, which Delage noticed was buttoned up, unusual inside a house. "I'm looking for our daughter. She's not here, I can see."

Towards the front of the queue the *Romance* waited at anchor, Delage, Elisabeth and the Dutchman at the rails, the English couple in plastic chairs fanning themselves, waiting as the line of ships came out of the canal, the opposite direction to theirs, slow and steady procession, container ships almost as large as theirs, others a quarter the size, green, gray, black, North African and Middle Eastern trading ships, dribbling rust, in need of paint. "They don't look after their things. They scratch out an existence from the soil, a subsistence, and let things go. They can be personally clean, they wash their hands before eating, they clean their teeth, sometimes using special twigs. What they then do is throw their rubbish and muck outside their windows, or into the ocean. Without science, they have no knowledge of hygiene," the Dutchman said. "And they wonder why others have trampled all over them. Because we are a tidy people," the Dutchman went on, "we have ruled the world." Elisabeth gave Delage a pinch, expecting him to say something. Then she'd turn away as if she wasn't listening, the way her mother did, in his cabin while the sun lit up her bare shoulders, he saw the fine blond hairs on her jaw, normally invisible. He had his elbow on the rail, the ship moving under his feet, which began to give the sensation his life was not moving forward, while the ship and everything else was. Midmorning they entered the canal, following three fat ships, traveling too slowly to produce a breeze. There was a simplicity to the straight line of the canal, which allowed the procession. His life had been a confusion, he found it difficult to express his views, let alone hold on to them, information and adjustments came in from all directions. Nothing was straightforward, not even the advantages of the Delage piano, it was not enough that the advantages were self-evident to him. Everybody has something to say, nobody is relaxed, too many things appear to be wrong in the world, every day there is something, the disappointments are of the ordinary kind; people close by end up ultimately as disappointments. It is only to be expected, the fit between people is never precise, each person becomes known by their differences, a practical tolerance comes to the fore, a social necessity, everyone has their opinions without the finer details, invariably getting it wrong or not quite right, being almost wrong or almost right, not many have the nerve to express themselves openly, unlike the Dutchman who for some time, he said, had been observing problems or faults without solutions, wherever he looked. One side of the canal was green or with patches of green, the other side sand the color of crumpled canvas, at set intervals a tin hut or booth with a young soldier sitting in it. Wreckage left rusting from a war, tank tracks, barbed wire, observation posts, turrets mangled and ripped, which interested the Dutchman and Delage, joined by the Englishman, more than it did Elisabeth. Hardly ever did another person agree with him, in his opinion, listen, look at it this way. And what difference have I made? Touching hips with Elisabeth, when there was plenty of room at the rail next to the Dutchman, a clear sign of intention, Elisabeth, it was where she wanted to be, he couldn't understand why. She was at least ten years younger than he was, something of his extra world-experience presumably showed. Her warmth blended into him, he recognized a comfort, a fact, not just familiarity. At the same time, he felt almost everything was beyond his reach. He decided to nudge, "You'll be seeing plenty of those where you're going, you'll get sick of the sight of them. Even the word will start to get you down. There's another one. Look, they're everywhere." Eucalypts were planted at intervals along the Suez Canal. "People in Europe say they're drab-looking." At this she took a closer interest, "They do not look healthy to me." "They can grow anywhere," Delage informed her. "They're adaptable—very. They remind me of you, the way you adapt." There she was, on a ship heading for Sydney, on the other side of the world. "Thank you very much. So now I am a tree." Below her ear along her sunlit jaw a surfeit of faint hairs flowed in one direction, bleached windswept grass, one afternoon south of Canberra (golden light); and he felt a sudden sympathy—for Elisabeth, with her unusual adaptability. The sisters from Melbourne had stayed below, missing the Suez Canal in its entirety, the younger one never married, the necessary signals had not come easily to her, there had been an absence of suitors, nobody could remember her conversing with a man, my sister, Delage couldn't help thinking, she was devoted to comforting her more worldly sister who spent a fortune on handbags, shoes and scarves, all her life she had preferred the company of men to women, attracted to their most intractable characteristics, a subject she could analyze with other women for hours at a time, she was an acknowledged expert, which hadn't prevented her husband of many years saying to himself, "Enough!" or not saying anything to himself at all, walking out the front door in Highgate, London, this was a few months earlier, leaving a typed note, a surprise to those who knew them both; and now after showing encouraging signs of being over the worst, the way sea air, sunlight and seagulls can increase an invalid's appetite, she had collapsed once again into the proverbial heap, as they entered the canal. She certainly couldn't be seen by the other passengers, she was unwell. In caring for her, the younger sister showed no concern for herself; a selfless woman, not interested in her appearance, aside from neatness. On the voyage they began to look more and more like identical twins than ordinary sisters, the fall in aura in one was met by a rise in energy and aura in the younger one, sharing between them a wariness in manner, in movement, dress, unsmiling speech. The straight line of the canal looked out of place in the sand: a human effort, an alteration. Nature prefers to follow the contours. Nature is lazy, it makes its own way. The Dutchman said to Delage, "I come from a horizontal country. The slightest movement is instantly noticed. We see things clearly. If Holland had mountains and valleys my wife would not have left me." Elisabeth whispered in Delage's ear that she came from a country of mountains, there's hardly a flat piece of land in all of Austria, she whispered, she wasn't about to run away, and the warm breath in her ear seemed to confirm it. She had arrived in the morning at the hotel in one of the family's Mercedes with chauffeur to take him on a tour of the city, "My mother no doubt thought you needed educating," looking at him closely. "She talked me into it. She didn't need to, really." A sudden smile. To Delage, she looked like difficulty, a troubled young woman. "Is your mother still speaking to me?" "And why wouldn't she be?" At that time, Delage found he was thinking about her mother, Amalia, altogether too much, he also thought, husband in tow, while her daughter displayed a shapely, careless attractiveness, taking him to every composer's house she could think of, especially if it included an antique piano, which it invariably did, as well as the gold-plated harp on its stand in the corner, beginning with Mozart's rooms behind the dark cathedral, it took all morning, many of the greatest composers lived and worked at some time in Vienna, often changing addresses. She had thought of everything, itself a statement of some kind. A corner table had been booked in a fancy restaurant. "My mother suggested we have lunch here. She is giving to you a lot of attention." And to join in, or outdo the power of her mother, Elisabeth von Schalla leaned forward, enticing Delage down to what lay waiting in shadow beneath her dress, the position of the chairs made it difficult for Delage to avoid. Delage became aware of certain familiar stages, which he knew were easily crossed. They shared a bottle of Moselle. "I should be doing the rounds of the piano people. Not that anyone's shown the slightest interest in what I have to say. I don't know what's the matter with the people in this place. Have their imaginations come to a grinding halt? Fossilized," he threw in for good measure. Elisabeth had no interest in pessimism, Delage had to be careful, even if he was exaggerating, he was doing his best not to dwell on her face, avoid the eyes, he assumed she didn't have a job of any sort, all the time in the world on her hands, an old phrase, he meant to ask what she did all day, it would have been fun showing a man from far away the hidden parts of her city. "I've been told to show you the house the philosopher Ludwig Wittgenstein designed. If you think our house is a mess, wait till you see this. He designed it for his sister." That was when Delage introduced his own sister who lived in Brisbane, explaining his irritation, it was more incomprehension than irritation. "Now there's a woman who never lets up. I don't know why she has to carry on," he said. She was always wanting to be involved in his life, while he wanted her to leave his life, or at least not be so involved. They crossed the Ringstrasse. "My mother admired Wittgenstein's intentions, but not the result. I think it would be like living in an office building. The Wittgensteins are related, on her side." It became difficult to concentrate, the idea of turning composers' houses into holy houses with perfect wallpaper, bare desk and polished floorboards is more a display of falsity than history, although it hardly deters the visitors who go into every room, wanting to add layers to their general knowledge, mouths open in wonder, in Mozart's case, amazing how a family with so many children could fit in such a space, how Mozart managed to work with his family around him, making the usual family racket, or the curator's immaculate recreation of Beethoven's rooms, not a speck of dust to be seen, when everybody knows he lived in disorder and squalor. According to Elisabeth, her mother contributed to the upkeep of the composers' houses, she even fought off Berthe Clothilde in an ugly public scene for the privilege. Naturally it concerned Delage that after three or four days no one had shown the slightest interest in his piano, aside from Amalia von Schalla, although her interest was not going to result in any sales. "I do not get much out of new sights. Once upon a time I did, yes. But new sights are hard to quantify, don't you think? What I miss is the unexpected," Amalia said, on the subject of travel, seated at one end of the low sofa. "I always enjoyed the discomfort of the unexpected. Surely that is good for the mind." To Delage, she had never talked as much, and hurriedly too, all because of the slap, he assumed. "It is different when traveling on business. The unexpected could prove a hindrance. What do you say?" "I'm here on business. It pays to keep the old eyes wide open, just in case." It had been difficult to get contacts, he needed just one door to be opened, one would be enough, the right door, even slightly open, not necessarily wide open, enough for him to step in, and after clearing his throat, launch into the advantages of the Delage piano. He discussed it on the sofa. "You have seen the piano, and I have explained it. Remember I played it for you. I put it through its paces. It was only a few days ago." He wanted to arrange a meeting with the music critic, even though his house with all his belongings had recently been burned to the ground. Delage thought she was thinking about something else. "Come back tomorrow evening. I should have an answer then." At the end of the canal they looked over the side as a pilot left the bobbing motor boat, leaped onto the ladder which had been lowered, and up to the bridge to direct the helmsman in a zigzag course through the lakes. "The captain tells me it is unnecessary, but it is the way they do things here." Also a custom was to give the pilot, who had a family to support, or even if he hadn't, a carton of American cigarettes: Delage wasn't watching as the man left the ship, the carton in one hand, he was thinking of Amalia von Schalla, what she would be doing back in Vienna, in her own uncluttered rooms, which he had a clear picture of, until blotted out by her face, a version of her face, filling rooms, when Elisabeth gave a cry. The pilot had fallen into the water, making a splash. Leaving him, the motor boat went to save the cigarettes which kept floating away. The German officers began shouting. The motor boat left the cigarettes and turned, everybody waving their arms and shouting, Elisabeth held on to Delage's arm, as the motor boat kept circling.

Once in the Red Sea where the heat and humidity gave Elisabeth a rash, nobody could recall the unfortunate pilot's face, he struck his head, the Dutchman had heard, only his white cotton shirt, wet hair, Elisabeth, at least ten years younger, stayed in the cabin, Delage doing his best lying on the bed to answer questions about his family, she showed little interest in the enormous, mostly vacant country she would soon be seeing, had no idea what she was letting herself in for. "I would not describe your time in Vienna as a failure. How could you possibly think it?" Yet she listened with only vague curiosity whenever he talked about the design of the Delage piano, and showed even less interest in, let alone concern for, his lack of success establishing it in Europe, as if career and income were of no importance. He was affable, yet dissatisfied. The sea looked warm, an oily slop. "It is definitely a different color," the Englishman leaning over the side, "possibly red." A habit of making appraisals had left the top of his face in a constant state of blinking, while the rest remained stationary, a man whose wife in the plastic chair hardly said a word, round, rosy, not keen on moving, especially in this heat. Hot meals still came to the table, heaps of carbohydrates, the requirement of seamen, Elisabeth pushing the plate away. The number of women in the British Empire who fainted in the heat would run into the thousands. "How the Romans managed without ice and soda water," the Dutchman said, reaching out for another serve, "is very impressive." He began talking about his wife, her tiredness, his wife became more and more tired. "It was a tiredness in general," he said, talking to no one in particular, "my wife began to move about slowly. She spoke more slowly. I was forced to wait. I did a lot of waiting. She wanted her tiredness to register. One day she said in a voice I could hardly hear she couldn't do up the buttons on her blouse. And before long our marriage became tired. Naturally I didn't think my wife had the strength to leave our marriage. I wish my wife hadn't left me, or I hadn't left her—whatever it was. We could have entered old age together, when I too would have been tired. It was the final period we might have shared." Plenty of people are in a state of irritation, every other person is unhappy about something. It is held in check. People learn to smile over nothing. Away from land the Dutchman found less to be irritated by, there was less detail, everything and everybody in his little country had been all too visible, even though his wife was nowhere to be seen, it had been easy on land to be irritated, there was always something, wherever he turned there was something not working, always something or somebody to react against. Either the world as he saw it was unsatisfactory, a mess, or he had become dislodged. He listened when Delage eventually told him about his piano. It had been left behind in Europe, in Vienna, "the musical center of the world." They had been having conversations, just the two of them, Delage doing most of the listening, the other man made him more thoughtful, he felt it, an unusual feeling—it didn't happen every day. Delage had always been drawn to people with clear ideas, he didn't mind standing alongside, some of what the Dutchman said was worth putting in his notebook. "If I hadn't been on board this ship," he said to Elisabeth, "I would not have met this interesting man." He waited for her to say, "There was me too," but she turned away slightly, a habit he had grown to like.

Ahead, behind and on either side, all water, a red-painted deck about six paces square, a long table dominated by an unnecessarily ornate candelabrum positioned in the center, the table so long the four sat at one end, von Schalla at the head, as required, Amalia and daughter facing Delage at the sides. "Elisabeth was good enough to show me the sights. There were so many it took the whole day." He looked at Konrad von Schalla, "Have you seen the place where Mozart lived?" Amalia wanted to hear what he thought of the rooms of the great composers, but her husband cut her off, "Tell me about your country. What has it given the world?" Delage had to think about that one, advances in agriculture and the Delage piano came to mind, he twisted his mouth to indicate he was thinking, someone's foot under the table began pressing against his, blurring any answers he may have had. "No composers, painters, novelists?" Amalia encouraged. "Not that I'm aware of," Delage shaking his head. Von Schalla went on eating the fish. "Our contribution," Delage still frowning, "has been in small areas, such as being relaxed, swimming in the sea—we grow strong teeth." Von Schalla threw his head back. "No products?"—he let out a laugh, and couldn't stop laughing. He pitched forward in a fit of coughing, which at first appeared to be a continuation of the laughing, but he clutched at his throat, his eyes bulging. He was turning dark red. Delage quickly tried thumping him between the shoulder blades. "A bone's got stuck in his throat. Relax!" he shouted, "keep still." Amalia and daughter looking on had their arms folded. It rained, stopped, rained again—pelting the ship as it passed through. When it stopped the clouds remained in place, filling the sky, ready to rain again, dark restless clouds, which darkened the air and sea. At intervals the ship crashed into a bigger wave, shuddering and creaking the plates. The entire ship awash, dribbling water, it ran down the windows of Delage's cabin. Off the Horn of Africa expect the weather to be foul, the captain telling them in passing. It's invariably rough in the Bay of Biscay too. Instead of bringing Delage and Elisabeth closer, the rain along with the noise and the poor light made them separate, keeping to themselves; Elisabeth lay without moving, not saying a word, she couldn't eat. There was nothing he could do. A few weeks remained before they would step ashore on the west coast of Australia, which has a history of visitors setting foot on the place and immediately wanting to turn around, a reaction which continues to this day, one of the disadvantages of living too close to warm blue water and mineral-bearing rocks, the number of concert grands in the entire state could be counted on one hand, Delage knew, Perth, sandy, sunlit capital, had developed a fragile, megalomaniac view of itself, the way local fishermen everywhere claim to have the best fish in the world, a visitor such as Elisabeth from the middle of Europe would quickly notice. Laugh aloud at even miniature forms of nationalism, the Dutchman had said. From Perth they could stay on the ship, take a few more days to reach modest Adelaide, or Melbourne, then fly to Sydney, he hadn't decided which, it depended on Elisabeth, he realized, he was interested in pleasing her, something else he realized. It was awkward returning empty-handed, having achieved virtually nothing in Europe, at least in a business sense, returning instead with a young woman from Vienna, and a slight change in personality, enough to take everybody by surprise, his sister in Brisbane most of all, she'd be on the first plane to give this Elisabeth, odd spelling, blond, she would have to be, on the surface representing good news, the once-over. As she went on sleeping, or lying still with her eyes shut, Delage could look down at her face, and remain looking, if he wanted to, Elisabeth unaware, or happy for him to gaze at every part, which took on the contours of a landscape, it happens when examining a sleeping face for any length of time, looking up from the chin especially, bare and hilly, smooth landscape. The first time he had seen her, Delage noticed her skin before anything else, she had her mother's fine skin. Other similarities were less visible. Elisabeth's mother was not like a mother at all, far from an ordinary mother, at least not one Delage had come across before, it didn't appear as if she'd ever carried a child, in Elisabeth's presence she was indifferent, she took more notice of Delage than her own daughter. They hardly looked at each other, Elisabeth could do whatever she liked. Whenever Delage looked at

Elisabeth, he thought of her mother, which was something he should try to stop. She had high cheekbones and a snub or tilted nose, which uplifted her face, unlike Elisabeth, who had a conventional, slightly large nose. It had taken several days for Amalia von Schalla to reach a comfortable smile, possibly a normal smile, it was almost imperceptible, out of politeness rather than reacting to anything funny he had said, before she thought better of it. By being strict with herself, Amalia had acquired a visual advantage; it was something else Delage could try to understand. Of the different smiles which appear in the world at any given moment, many have no meaning, the reflex or shopkeeper's smile, the half-smile, the quarter-smile, and smaller, the foolish smile, we smile to ourselves when there's nobody to see, the one of recognition sent across a distance (a street) is almost spontaneous, in regular use is the short-distance smile to narrow a social gap, a proven conversation aid, no more than that. So much insincerity around the smile, so much sincerity. It is also true, as the statisticians point out, that women smile more readily, especially being photographed, Amalia being an exception. "Speed was the essence. At other times it is not," von Schalla said in a hoarse voice. "First decide when to move, and then at what speed. It applies when you buy, and if you have something to sell. You did well." Delage was standing with his hands in his pockets, von Schalla stretched out on the bed in perfectly pressed English pajamas, his head supported by square pillows; with flat edges like padded envelopes, the same as in his hotel, these are continental pillows; they slept in separate rooms, Delage noted.

Von Schalla went on to say he had never been partial to fish, unlike women who insist on eating fish three times a week for the good of their figures, there would inevitably be a problem with a stray bone, which was just another reason to be "more interested in meat and Austrian sausage." He'd had a scare. He was left with a sparrow's complexion. "You sprang into action," von Schalla was commending. "Decisive. Would I have done the same?" Exceptionally compact in a well-cut suit, he was diminished in pajamas. Again, so many dark objects in every direction, even here, a bedroom. "I'm all over the place at the moment," Delage told Amalia—meaning his life. Too many objects around him, too many unexpected things happening. On the opposite wall was an important portrait of a man wearing a high military collar and a cold smile, steel engravings of old Vienna, two marble obelisks on the mantelpiece, ornate clock, pieces of pewter serving no purpose, gold-and-crimson chairs, dressing gown over another, pair of black shoes, desk on delicate legs, briefcase (wide open), a door ajar revealing a bathroom. Von Schalla pointed, "On top of the desk there, hand me those drawings. Thank you. These are Egon Schiele drawings." He handed them back to Delage, about a dozen, nudes of the same scrawny woman, hollow cheeks, legs wide apart. "I want you to choose one. Take it." Nothing was said for a few minutes, Delage didn't like the look of the drawings. "I see you hesitating. It is wise to take care. Some years ago a man came to this house to see me. As he waited downstairs a young woman arrived from a hospital. She was agitated. The man said, 'Let me see.' She thought: who is this? How impertinent.

But she handed him the X-rays of herself, of her body, not knowing who he was. He examined the images of her. I am told he said, 'You should relax. You are not relaxed.' The young woman was Amalia, about to be my wife. She didn't know she had been disloyal. The man worked in our stables, shoveling manure, as his father had done before him. These people are mostly stupid. He turned out to have a few brains. I put him through medical school. On occasion I am happy to be generous. Sometimes it suits me, or it does not. He lives a short distance away, on Theobaldgasse. I receive excellent medical service, as you would have observed."

It was complicated enough in Vienna without Delage having to hear a story that had nothing to do with him or pianos, even if every story told is interesting in its own way, a story of little apparent consequence possesses its own momentum, its own permanence, however slight, von Schalla turned at Delage's hesitation and was looking at him. "Take a drawing by our Schiele. I insist." Often when Delage was due to see somebody he would think ahead to what to say and how to speak, his first words, his middle words, be prepared for the effect they might have, although nothing had prepared him for Konrad von Schalla, of the von Schalla dynasty, stretched out on the bed, thin, pint-sized, back all the way to the Dark Ages, subtle and insistent, these layerings of old Europe, be careful, unembarrassed in pajamas, which indicated a natural arrogance, now bearing gifts. "I have been meaning to ask—do you happen to know the Steinway agent in Vienna? Would he, by any chance, be sabotaging my efforts?" The doors remained closed, he wanted to say, so much for free trade, no wonder the place was grinding to a halt; and he saw it would be all too easy to slip into von Schalla's debt. "Sabotage?" von Schalla turned the word over several times. "I hardly think so. It would not be necessary for Steinway." He went on thinking about the question. "What I would say is, should you need assistance, stay away from your embassy. They will do harm, and no good. There is not a commercial mind there. Mediocre people like nothing better than to work in the embassies. Their most accomplished skills are pouring cocktails and stamping passports." In a distracted way she allowed him to place his hand on her hip, Amalia, in her rooms, austere stylish furniture and walls matching her. If the paintings and furnishings said she was modern, she wouldn't mind, Delage assumed, he moved his hand to the small of her back, kept it there, waiting for a sign, encouragement in the form of a lean, a stillness, not necessarily a word. "He asked if I would dine here tomorrow night." "But of course. You saved his life, I saw it myself. And what did you say?" "It would make three evenings in a row, I said." She turned, dropping his hand, "What does that have to do with it? Elisabeth would like you here, that I know. If there are other sights you would like to see during the day, she will take you. There are palaces outside the city." Delage began pacing, "I haven't done a thing. I need to see people, and the right people. And soon. I don't know what's been happening. I have made no headway. Berlin would have been a better bet. At least I have some serious introductions for Berlin." Aside from inventing and manufacturing a new piano, he was not expert at anything else, nothing he could think of, certainly not the job of salesman selling a concert grand to, of all places, musical Europe, he'd do better in Taiwan or parts of the Middle East, even then he wouldn't be comfortable. In his teens, Delage was prone to stammer because of talking and talking, his thoughts getting ahead of his words, until it went. One day he stammered, the next day did not. Traces remained until he embarked on piano design and construction, which required very little talking. She took his hand, "The poor man, our music critic, who you saw giving the talk. You can introduce your wonderful new piano to him. I will arrange it for tomorrow." Such sympathy was at odds with her appearance, it was something else he could not understand, kindness, attentiveness, sympathy were qualities to be found in women, their defining qualities for him, in recent times becoming scarce. The ordinariness of people, of everyday events, had resulted in an ordinary world; it had reduced him to ordinariness, Delage, he could feel it, as he left Europe. His sister in Brisbane would say he was not ordinary enough, he was too extraordinary, which allowed only a small space for the ordinary others to approach and be close, all our family are extraordinary, she was fond of saying, we are different, meaning herself, leaving little room for someone to fit with her. In the face of the most formidable obstacles he had produced a grand piano at such a distance from the ordinary it attracted little interest from the majority. Approaching the Malaccas it was so hot Elisabeth went about naked, strolling as if the cabin was a large bathroom, bending over, happy for him to watch, then she was on the bed, legs apart, at the most awkward angles, aware of her body, it became a drop of water bulging from a tap, a move from him and it would disintegrate. “Tell me again about your meeting with the music critic,” she asked. “How did he react to your piano?” Lying on her stomach, her bare legs waving about in the air, Elisabeth was safe, the metal of the ship surrounding her, while he remained, tolerant, she didn’t need to fully listen to his answer. The Dutchman had not appeared for meals, Delage knocked on his door, he was not ill, “thank you for the inquiry,” he was rearranging his life beginning with his room, the cabin, it was taking longer than he thought, he said, it had become essential to clear his mind. There must be as few obstacles to thought as possible. Among his plans of beginning afresh was settling in Australia, at least have an open mind on the idea, he could easily be repelled by the place, as the early Dutch explorers had been, he would never have thought of going to Australia if it hadn’t been for the small library of rare exploration books he was delivering, he would give Australia serious consideration once he had stepped ashore, Perth was a possibility, nothing would be excluded, not even the interior where he assumed there would be small towns, these days you can set up a bookshop in a tin shed, perhaps one specializing in voyages and exploration, as long as there was electricity. “Only stupid people are amazed,” the Dutchman said, a quote interesting enough for Delage to think of people, beginning with himself, who were amazed, and later he wrote it down. Being on the ship as it goes along, Delage said to Elisabeth, we’re going with the general flow, it’s the way we live. There were pauses when nothing much happened, the surprises, occasional discomforts, going forward whether they wanted to just then or not. It's not necessarily a good feeling. After Elisabeth had rested her chin on her hand with interest, Delage then said the same thing to the sisters, who could only talk about the collapse of the elder sister's marriage, she was never going to be the same, she was an altered woman, the younger one doing her best to be patient and sympathetic, "cut adrift" was her description, a nautical term, when they took meals together the elder one looking quite unwell, at the same time, determined, all those years had been wasted years, her first reaction, the younger one smiling and shining, a kind person, so much so that when the Englishman's wife turned her sympathy onto the pair, it was not needed (politely ignored).

As soon as he sat down in the back, squashing Delage against Elisabeth, he wriggled the way a concert pianist settles on his stool, at the same time clearing his throat noisily, it was obvious he was the famous music critic, the residue of smoke in his clothing was immediately noticeable, the chauffeur swung around in his seat to see if the upholstery or something was burning. Delage went to shake his hand, "It was decent of you to come. I appreciate it." This was the hand that had ruined the careers of promising violinists and sopranos, and hoisted others to unsustainable heights, an almost magical hand, if it was the actual one which had written his implacable judgments, critics have an absurd sense of their own superiority, an art critic can be found writing film criticism (it's visual), or even literary criticism, music critics feel they can turn their hand to theater criticism, or criticism of architecture or town planning, they suffer from a constant psychological condition which constantly prompts them to be critical—nothing can be done about it, a critic begins as a failure. Ignoring Delage's hand, the critic turned to Elisabeth, "Your mother has been very generous, as always." He whistled through his teeth a few bars from Mahler. He had a natural talent for expressive whistling, something Delage never had. "Aside from anything else," he said, "piano is not my favorite sound. We will see what is so important for me to cross Vienna for." "I thought it was you who said what is new is important. Unless I didn't hear correctly," Delage said. The critic actually laughed, "So you remembered? You would be the only one that night who did." It felt unusual, squashed in the back knowing Amalia von Schalla had arranged the meeting, she didn't have to do it, whether it was for him or a love of music he could not decide, a combination probably, nothing is one. Delage often thought about people's motives, he was especially interested in Amalia's, whose presence was represented by her only daughter, Elisabeth, pressed hard against him in the dark limousine, she didn't talk much, but then nor did her mother. To his surprise, the critic began asking about Australia. They were not questions about the musical world, although he couldn't help shaking his head at the Sydney Opera House, which Delage's sister insisted on visiting whenever she came down from Brisbane, it had the worst acoustics of any opera house in the world, according to the critic from Vienna, it is typical of the New World to prefer appearances over substance, "they ought to pull it down, and start again," he said, he only wanted to know about the dangerous spiders and sharks that infested Australia, and the snakes, how lethal were they really; had Delage ever seen a live snake writhing on the ground? Dozens more people in Australia die of thirst or from bushfires than snakes or sharks, Delage wanted to say. What a country! In one way or another all are terrible, every country. "A country far away from everywhere else, and you tell me you have designed and built your own piano?" "Everything's new in my country," Delage explained. He wanted to say to Elisabeth, "Your mother isn't very happy, it seems to me." But pressed between her and the smoke-drenched music critic, although there was plenty of room, he thought he should commiserate, or at least show an interest, and ask if he'd lost everything in the fire. "I thought it was history beginning all over again. I have a small amount of Jewish blood, you see. I am left with the clothes I am standing in. That is all I need." Looking at the music critic as he spoke, Delage saw there was much in him to like. Here was a man who had just lost all his possessions, all his papers, copies of all his reviews and notes for them in plastic bags, books, benchmark recordings, mattress, nothing left but the black shirt and tight trousers he was standing in, and perhaps cutlery, a few plates, knives and forks can survive, who was now looking at the passing trees and buildings, glancing up at the clouds, as if he had never been in a car before, not cursing or brooding over his recent misfortune, he was whistling in fits and starts a few more bars, a remarkable rendition of Webern, Ligeti, one or the other. It can be seen as a fresh beginning, he said. A composer begins with thin air. "Everything is before me, all over again. I am talking about the fact of the situation. I have nothing to complain about." So lost in admiration was Delage, he was unaware his hand had settled on Elisabeth's knee. She was lying on her side, leaning on her elbow, one hip rearing in assertive womanly abundance, the ship's engine underneath and forward motion faintly shifting her breasts. "I wonder what your mother is doing in Vienna right now?" "She does not know where I am. I am thirty-six years old. What are we going to do in Sydney?" "You might not like the place. After five minutes you might want to scoot back home." The very thought was enough for her to drape her hand around his neck, such was happiness or contentment on the container ship, easy to be with, Elisabeth von Schalla, no difficulties or awkwardness, he didn't have to watch each and every step, take care what he said or didn't say, he felt he could say anything at all. With Elisabeth he could breathe easily, her mother was like this too. The English married couple had been arguing on the small deck, rather, the Englishman was heard raising his voice, none of the other passengers felt they could venture onto the small deck, the woman said nothing, pink from top to toe, it was not the first time she had been shouted at, they could tell from the deck below. The elbow of one of the two sisters now cut across Delage's field of vision, the sisters sitting together, the one whispering to the disconsolate older one had begun brushing her hair, it was rich chestnut-dyed, a portrait of sisterly devotion if ever there was, the methodical brushing by the smaller, possibly younger, sister almost immediately smoothed out the haggard look on the inconsolable one, a comfort can give hope, Delage observed. Nothing lasts, at least not in original form. "She is going to be alright," Elisabeth's view at a glance. The one being brushed didn't want her sister to be her best friend, she wanted more. "I'll see what's happened to the Dutchman," Delage announced. Elisabeth had her foot pressed firmly on the top of his shoe in full view of the music critic, if he chose to look down, not shoes exactly, Delage wore boots with a well-oiled worn look, made in Tasmania. They'd left the museum area behind, heading toward the warehouse district, Delage thought he recognized corners and streets. What promised to be a turning point in the future of the Delage piano was delayed by the critic who tapped the chauffeur on the shoulder when he saw a shop specializing in sausage; Delage and Elisabeth remained seated, together they watched as he leaned forward over the gutter, taking bites out of the dark sausage, Bertolt Brecht photographed struggling to light one of his cheap cigars, Elisabeth's foot remaining on Delage's boot. She went ahead of the two men at the piano warehouse, the critic contemplating her from behind, at the same time managing to talk while finishing the last of the sausage—an example of the true independence necessary to the critic. He said he often had seen her mother, Amalia von Schalla, across the room, as he put it, the number of musical events he was required to attend in a given week was truly staggering, it played havoc with his diet, his sleep patterns, his own social life had become nonexistent, he was always being asked to attend something arranged by others, Amalia von

Schalla made her requests sparingly, as a consequence was doubly, possibly triply, effective. Naturally when Amalia von Schalla asked would he be so kind as to give this new piano from Australia a hearing he canceled all other appointments and requests to comply. In Vienna she was the most important patron of music, he told Delage more than once, a great help to composers and hopeful conductors, she even threw money at the Vienna Boys' Choir, which may be a successful export but was a ridiculous embarrassment to musical Vienna. "Mother and daughter," the critic said, "one is C major, the other A minor. I've just this minute thought of that," he said, as they entered the building, Delage looking more closely at the shape ahead of them. Later, when Elisabeth asked what they were talking about back there, Delage shook his head. For some time he had been trying to see the world a step removed from musical terms, in thoughts and conversations he had caught himself bringing everything back to the Delage piano, or the scarcity of skilled labor, or the music business in general, mentioning the advantages of his piano at every opportunity. It was a wonder his sister had not pointed this out, although she may well have said it by other means. A lot of what she said went clean over his head. He would listen carefully now to what he himself said. To go about doing the hard-sell on the Delage piano was counterproductive. Naturally people in power begin to have doubts if they detect anxiety in someone giving a pitch. It was a building of metal doors. Behind the offices in the storage area a man came and switched on the lights. At the sight of so many parked pianos in rows with narrow aisles, the critic stretched out his arms and said something in German. Elisabeth translated, "An elephants' graveyard." "Ah, yes," Delage joining in, "the ivory." Elisabeth was shapely, expensive, leaning against the rail above the steps, waiting for them. In many small ways she reminded him of her mother, Delage leading the way through the different concert grand pianos, before reaching his own toward the far end. As he whipped off the dust-sheet, Elisabeth alongside, he remembered he had made a similar theatrical flourish for Amalia von Schalla, a few days earlier. And it was here, when he was first alone with Amalia, his hand had gone forward in an involuntary manner, out of control, she allowed him to touch her.

It was not a matter of doing the hard-sell, it was simply a matter of introducing his piano—that was all. Neither the critic nor Elisabeth seemed to mind the yellow-brown color. He flicked some dust off the lid with his handkerchief, lifted the lid to explain the technical advantages of the Delage piano, there were quite a few, they could be seen only by peering in, he could point to them easily. The critic was not interested. "Play it," he shook his head, "play it, so I can hear." To give a recital in front of the leading music critic in Vienna was known to be a terrifying prospect, the most accomplished and experienced soloists froze, or made elementary blunders, or even vomited, his career-ruining pronouncements were taken as gospel in Vienna, in Berlin too, the most music-drenched cities in Europe, where the piano was said to be in decline anyway. Delage's playing was not good enough for him to be nervous, his skill rudimentary, if that. In his work it was not necessary for him to actually play music. He also couldn't decide from his repertoire what he should play, as he adjusted the stool, although it didn't need adjustment, out of the corner of his eye he could see the critic becoming impatient. Elisabeth too he saw now leaning with her elbows on top of the piano, watching him with concern. The strange falseness of the situation gave Delage a feeling of carelessness, which made him relax. Delage began with scales. A person with a basic knowledge of music would hear how the progression of notes of the Delage piano was immediately clearer, sharper than all the other concert grands. The critic began to speak rapidly in German, complaining that listening to somebody playing scales was useless, he could not form a clear picture, only a mechanical device with ears, as he put it, could, he began blowing his nose in irritation, this wasn't a Dada event, he said, the trip across Vienna in the traffic had been a waste of time, he was sorry and so on, while Delage continued up and down the scales, half turning to give explanations over his shoulder. The difficulty was the music critic himself could not play the piano, violin, yes, but not piano; he had never been keen on the piano, making a move for the exit. Compared to the violin, even the viola, certainly the cello, it was a shallow instrument. At this point, Elisabeth slid alongside Delage on the stool, as if she were slipping into bed, he said to her later, removing his hand from the keyboard, and began to play softly, a Schubert sonata, which stopped the critic in his tracks, then Scriabin, Schoenberg to and fro, all of which, although hardly to concert standard, allowed the critic to close his eyes, listen carefully. The way the wind changed: constantly, rapidly, it was indicated by the waves. At a glance the officers could measure the wind to a scale. They had established a hierarchy of winds. It was taking too long for Delage to reach home, he was restless to have his feet back on solid ground, otherwise he had little interest in Singapore, the Dutchman standing at the rail. "My father had about him the leftovers of cloves and other tropical spices. In Amsterdam he dressed in cotton jackets and bush shirts. He grew up in the Dutch East Indies, as they were called. The changing of place names has been a nuisance to school teachers and of course a bonanza to publishers of maps. Every other week you'll notice another country or city has decided to change its name. If a person said Zimbabwe, or Mumbai, or Beijing, my father gave the impression he didn't know what was meant. Sometimes he put his hand to his ear, as if he was deaf. All through what he continued to call Java were towns and villages, and rivers too, he no longer recognized." In the darkness on either side were small lights, some moving. As the ship slowed and approached the dock, the air became thick and sweet, uncomfortably humid. Most changes are larger than the person complaining about them, nothing at all can be done, so much is out of reach. Delage leaned against Elisabeth's shoulder, "When the sun decides to come up, we'll step ashore. I have a few things to do—postcards. I don't want my sister slashing her wrists. I should phone the office. I'll tell them more about the sale. After that we'll sit in a cane chair under a ceiling fan. I've had nothing but good reports on the Singapore

Sling." On the way back from the piano warehouse, the music critic said nothing, he sat with them in the spacious car, Elisabeth, Delage, without saying a word, instead of giving his considered opinion in the car, which could make or break the prospects of the Delage piano, he said nothing, eventually he began playing a tune on his knee with his fingers, which could only mean he had come to a conclusion, still he remained silent, it wasn't clear if he had a good or bad opinion of the piano that had come all the way from Sydney, Australia. He sat on his hands, as it were. He had seen too much opera, the art of the drawn-out conclusion, theater is dependent on cheap tricks, people pay for absurdly expensive tickets in order to experience cheap tricks, the operatic principle is one of delay, the drama of withholding, denying the audience to stretching point, and so leaving them aghast and breathless, clutching at the sides of their seats, waiting for the dénouement, dabbing the eyes, even when they've seen it many times before. And Delage and Elisabeth squashed together could only remain patient, although Delage was tempted to ask abruptly for the verdict, the silence was not promising, almost certainly a bad sign. Outside the Café Schwarzenberg, he asked the driver to stop, at the same time motioned Delage to step out, "on the footpath, he talked to me for five minutes," he told them at the Schallas' main table, Konrad von Schalla at the head, Amalia next to him, Delage, Elisabeth opposite her, "people had to walk around us on the footpath, as he delivered his verdict." The bare shoulders of both mother and daughter were soft in the candlelight. It must have been Elisabeth who gently kicked his foot under the table. "What he had to say was interesting, I've been thinking about it ever since. It had taken him a while to see what the problem was. The sound of the Delage piano, he said, was too pure. Unlike a Steinway or a Bösendorfer the tone was not blurry, it was a new sound, clean and precise. It is what I have always said. But he said it doesn't allow for imperfections. A person playing the Delage piano would be exposed with every note. It is unforgiving. And that would be alright, except it was not a technical mistake, it showed a misunderstanding of art—he said 'catastrophic misunderstanding.' All art, he said, including the playing of pianos, was imperfect. He went on to say, quite loudly on the footpath, the power of art did not come from perfection, but in the demonstrated effort—he emphasized 'effort'—of creation. As listeners, we actually want an imperfect result. It is human, and therefore closer to human understanding. Otherwise, it is beyond understanding. He finished by saying that whoever invented such a perfect piano would be just as unforgiving in his life. That was something that hadn't crossed my mind," Delage gave a quick laugh. There was silence at the table. Either the Schalla family was absorbing the critic's verdict, or they had trouble understanding it, or they were expressing sympathy to Delage. It could also have been they didn't care either way, his world was one they didn't inhabit. "Something else he made very clear," Delage continued. "My piano is not about to make any headway in Europe, because the classical composers have written for the European blurry tone. They have made good use of it. Brahms, he mentioned. The only hope, your critic said, would be in contemporary music. Some of the new composers might take an interest. The precise tone could suit their cold compositions. Otherwise," said Delage, "I might as well pack up and go home." Close to Amalia, he was aware of being aware of himself, and with it uncertain of the merits of his piano. To avoid Amalia, he turned to Elisabeth, who gave him a smile. "Contemporary composers can always be commissioned," her mother said. "However much they protest," von Schalla from the end, "they like nothing better than to hang around the salons, eating from our table. Prokofiev ate like a horse, in this very house." "Berthe has three young composers under her wing," Amalia recalled. Delage went on cutting up the schnitzel using the family silver, the knives and forks had handles made from antlers. "Am I hanging around, as you put it? I don't think so." "You are silly," Elisabeth leaned forward, "you are not a composer." "A manufacturer," von Schalla agreed, or appeared to agree, whenever possible his face wanted to express reserve. Composers and artists were drawn inexorably to the old families, such as the Schalla family, wealth and casual influence dazzled them, artists especially, all those walls waiting to be filled with their canvases, watercolors, sculptures, experimental photographs, their creations secured ahead of all others. If they learned that a patron, or a possible patron, had an interest in waterfalls or tulips it wasn't long before they arrived with a painting of one, just for your interest, under their arm. There is always a salesman aspect to the artist, part of their anxiety. At least with a painting, the patron ended up with something to be displayed, or put to one side, a tangible asset that could one day rise in value, whereas if a composer is commissioned the patron is lucky to have in minuscule type a dedication printed on the score. And just as the old families would let drop that a composer or the painter so-and-so had been around for afternoon tea, in the conservatory, so too would the composer or the painter reveal they had once again been invited to the Schallas' for pastries and coffee. "Patronage is nonexistent where I come from," Delage told them. "I'm not complaining," he added. Something bothered him at the table, Amalia looking straight ahead, her daughter glancing at him. If it was Elisabeth whose foot had given the little kick, it was still pressing against his. Whenever he moved, it followed. "Don't be hasty," came von Schalla's advice—from a master-businessman, enough for Amalia to unfold her hands on the napkin. Von Schalla held a steady, not unfriendly gaze, which seemed to encourage Delage still trying to come to terms with the critic's verdict, the future of his piano in Europe was limited at best, Vienna, he could see now, had been the worst possible place to introduce an improvement to something as long-established as the grand piano, some things are resistant to change, in Vienna their sausage, sauerkraut and pastries were beyond improvement too. It had been a difficult day for Delage, although he ended up liking the music critic, who gave the impression, without coming out and saying it, not in so many words, they could meet up again, perhaps at the Café Bräunerhof, the homeliest of the cafés, where, he said, the most irritable men in Vienna sat and read their newspapers, the world after all consisted of hundreds of constantly shifting irritations, which was why the Bräunerhof had become his second home, the world was composed of nothing but irritations, he touched Delage's elbow, we can only do our best, it was a comfort to be surrounded at the Café Bräunerhof by others who either openly expressed their irritation at the world around them, or allowed unspoken irritation to develop in their faces, irritation being a sign of intelligence, there nevertheless was always a quiet corner, they could have their coffee and pastries, while he asked for more details of the deadly insects, reptiles and fish of Australia. But Delage had only a week or so left in Europe, before catching the container ship at Hamburg. And he was also trying to work out where the difficulty lay at the table. From where he was seated, he could hardly avoid Amalia's throat and bare shoulders, by leaning at a slightly different angle he could include her daughter's expanse of candle-white softness, as she bent forward, Elisabeth, helpfully. In the space between Amalia, who had long pale hands, just the one diamond ring, and her blue-eyed daughter, there were no clear signs, nothing he recognized or could follow in confidence. He wasn't sure what he was offering these people. He had the feeling he could spend the rest of his life in a warm room talking, or listening, sometimes stepping out with one of them. Von Schalla was now talking, "I suppose in your business you become a connoisseur. Have you heard our daughter play at the piano?" Elisabeth gave one of her faint smiles, which made Delage smile. "She stepped forward today and saved the situation—didn't you? I see you're being modest." "Unfortunately, it was my playing that made up the critic's mind. I have never really liked that man." "For a brief time, we were hoping for a concert career. Weren't we, darling?" Elisabeth turned from her mother. "It was never my intention," she said, "I knew I was not good enough." "Where to now?" von Schalla asked Delage. "Is it possible our famous critic has got it wrong?" Appearing thoughtful, Delage began shaking his head. "You have come from a long distance, only to be given bad news. We are sorry," Amalia said to Delage, and gave a little tap on his sleeve with her finger, Elisabeth observing her mother's sympathy, Delage's gratitude. It was interesting to see her mother at work. Partly because her distant beauty and manner were shared by people who came in contact with her, Elisabeth couldn't imagine this woman as her own mother. And she saw how the combination of opposites, elusive beauty offering sympathy, exerted an unexpected power, of which her mother was oblivious. For herself, Elisabeth had a more modern approach: a woman had nothing whatsoever to apologize for. "The piano is only a mechanical construction overlaid on nature," Delage had written in his notebook, no longer sure whether it came from the opinionated music critic back in Vienna, or the difficult Dutchman on the ship. "It's the sort of idea either of them could have come out with," he said to Elisabeth, "I could always ask the one nearest." "Our own private Dutchman," Elisabeth in her clipped voice. "Anyway, what you have written can apply to practically anything manufactured." They were sitting on the small deck. She was wearing a yellow blouse, pink linen trousers, nothing underneath. "Do you have written observations about me? Show me." For several days no other ships were sighted. Not only had the Englishman tried to reserve his own chair, the green plastic one, placing it carefully for himself in the same position on the small deck the way the British claimed tropical islands for their empire, he made a practice of stepping out at mid-morning in pajamas and dressing gown, as if the *Romance* was not a German container ship but the royal yacht *Britannia*, wearing pajamas outside cabins naturally was frowned upon, at that hour or any hour, until the captain requested he wear ordinary clothing, even though he or the officers rarely came onto the small deck, after which the Englishman, at every opportunity, gave impersonations of the captain including horizontal hand movements and his Bavarian accent. A rectangle of dense shadow divided the deck, where the sisters sat in any chairs available, out of their cabin into the full glare of the world, almost touching the other passengers seated in their chairs, a small congested part of the world, the younger sister careful to keep her older sister, who was not wearing make-up, itself a statement of some sort, away from the direct sun. "She's coming along, I think she's going to be alright," the younger one whispered, her sister was looking the other way. "It's happened to all of us," the Englishwoman to Elisabeth, said as a warning, women everywhere, the softness of her face momentarily disappearing. "I don't have a clue what to say to her," Delage admitted later. It wasn't that he disliked the Englishwoman, he didn't know what to say, with his sister too, he often became stuck for words. "She never stops smiling, it's hard to concentrate when someone's always smiling. And what does it mean? When she does talk, it's about the weather." Some people are addicted to knowing about the weather, the present and future weather reports, it stands for something else. "Unhappy woman," said Elisabeth. It was too hot on the other side of the great sloping funnel, they had crossed the Equator in darkness, Delage pointed to flying fish, small islands attracted larger clouds, the gray-green, almost black immensity of the ocean, now the Indian Ocean.

And as von Schalla led him away from the table, Delage glanced at Amalia, her daughter opposite, pale women seated, Amalia folded her napkin once again, then folded her hands, Elisabeth looking up at Delage, an expression of calm. Here von Schalla's breast-pocket handkerchief resembled two or three protruding white envelopes, containing checks, dark suit obviously tailored in London buttoned up, as always, it made him appear alert, ready to spring with unconventional rapidity—he'd leap in behind a dozy management and onto the share registry when least expected, spreading apprehension in boardrooms across all of Europe. So far Delage had had nothing but friendliness from von Schalla. The blue-eyed Austrian would have placed a grateful hand on his shoulder, if only he had been tall enough, he had the greatest respect for inventors, "as a sub-species," his words. "If it were not for brains like you, we would still be up in the trees." With bankers he showed no mercy when it came to using them, their skill, such as it was, consisted of nothing more than allowing money to pass through their hands, each time peeling off a percentage, the caution, the lack of invention, it can be seen too in the novel these days, which no longer stands as invention, more and more an author's reaction to nearby events, a display of true feeling. And when the world was busily inventing things with moving parts, for the convenience of everybody else, there were large numbers of Frank Delage types bent over drawing boards and work benches, but now that most things had long been invented and were running like clockwork, the restlessly inventing type had become rare, in Europe there were hardly any left at all. Von Schalla regarded Delage not as a businessman from Sydney, but a visiting-inventor from the Southern Hemisphere, a practical man who had possibly saved him from choking to death, he would never forget that, although Delage had not given it another thought, an inventor was accustomed to using his hands, in all circumstances. "I have something for our visitor to see," Amalia stood up. Von Schalla gave a slight bow. "You are in demand." "Ten o'clock tomorrow," Elisabeth whispered as she brushed past, "I'll collect you at the hotel." In Vienna, Delage had been doing more observing than talking, in the dining room of the Schalla house there was much to take in, moments to comprehend, the impressions waiting to be classified, often conflicting, he was not accustomed to having the many different layers before him; and when he did say something, he felt no awkwardness with Amalia, or her daughter, or with the multinational businessman, Konrad von Schalla. In fact, when Delage spoke it came out in a series of abrupt rushes, almost careless in his deployment of words. He was following Amalia down the corridor, the businessman von Schalla at his side. The scratches and scuff marks on the skirting boards displayed, on the surface, a casual attitude to property, old money demanding satisfaction in appearances, relaxed in the details, as long as the comfort was there. "Be decisive, but not hasty. Always leave yourself room," came the businessman's advice, which could apply to situations other than selling pianos. In every village and town in Europe, ambitious entrepreneurs would have given anything to spend five minutes at the feet of Konrad von Schalla, and here he was giving a master class in coldness, business acumen in general, to Frank Delage, not from Austria, Australia, close in product-name but entirely different, Australia being far beyond the horizon, an invisible country of no consequence, Delage, who hadn't sought von Schalla's business advice, listened to what he had to say about women, or rather, Amalia. It was doubtful, by the way, that Delage could read sheet-music. They were following Amalia. "My wife was always shapely," he said. "I always liked the look of her. Whether she has ever felt the same way about me I am not sure." "Have you asked her?" "What?" Von Schalla paused at the door. "Where do you get these impractical ideas from? A small area in the back of your brain, allocated to 'hopeless and impractical ideas'—or what? Excuse me." He said something in German to his wife, waiting at her door. "Men of short size have a clearer view of women," as if talking to himself, taking a key from his coat pocket and opening his door, "that is my opinion. It is in the design of woman to be constantly changing their hair, dresses, perfume and shoes to give men the illusion they are always with a different woman, so keeping the man for themselves. My wife has cupboards full of dresses and shoes." He switched on the light. "How long has your company making the pianos been in business?" In Europe, people had so many extraordinary thoughts, and didn't mind saying them, Delage wondered whether his new piano was extraordinary at all. "I was about to show you my private art collection. Another time." By remaining at the door, Delage indicated a loyalty to the neatly dressed businessman, whom he barely knew, if he closed his eyes he would have had trouble describing him, aside from the externals, silver hair, the small shoes, which were unimportant, now they shook hands, a loyalty different in feeling from his loyalty to Amalia, which was not loyalty at all, she had closed her door, he noticed, more a spreading attraction, made stronger by a focus difficult to avoid; it included her daughter as well, Elisabeth, a woman displaying a younger sort of patience, almost a form of mockery, she had her own room down the other end of the house, perhaps on another floor. Since the invention of central heating, families have become dispersed, even in small houses. On the green sofa, Delage leaned forward and examined his palms, thinking it would interrupt the momentum taking him toward her, almost touching already, Amalia von Schalla, by transferring the attention to him, specifically a part of him, possibly his hands. When he came in she was seated, as if granting an audience; she patted a place beside her, which he took. He felt at ease going forward and sitting alongside, but immediately began looking at his hands. Amalia bent over and looked at them too. "They are not the hands of a pianist, I am told." He held his stumpy fingers up to the light and seemed to agree.

"I've come to a dead end with the piano," not quite changing the subject. Instead of taking an interest, she suddenly stood up, it was to her advantage, some women are better seated, Amalia better standing, straight-backed, poise producing a certain distance. Without moving, she appeared to be doing a slow dance. Delage got to his feet too. "Did he show you his collection? I wish he would not." Delage shook his head. "I didn't go in." Standing near Amalia, he became unsure, not wanting to stumble, his sister would have had a theory on that, she had a theory for anything he did or didn't do, she read a lot of women's magazines, perhaps for this purpose, he could hear her flipping the pages even when she was on the phone to him. The hand he placed on her hip moved, after a pause, to her breast, or almost, stopped, he didn't want to take advantage. It was hardly the moment to bring the subject back to himself, to the simple fact of his disappointing piano. In Amalia, he saw a brief affinity to the Steinways, Bechsteins, Bösendorfers gathering dust in silent rooms in Vienna, their lids closed, like Europe itself, a place hardly able to breathe, a matter of raising the glossy black lids, waiting to release sounds. At least Amalia had made an attempt, in private she was demonstrating to herself an alternative. The walls were white, the geometry in the paintings suggested a modern moment, as of now, which happened to match or be in tune with the new sound of his piano. With just a few days to go in Vienna, he had to chalk up some success, yet instead of making valuable contacts, seeking introductions, using the phone, here he was merging in warmth with the aristocratic woman who alone had tried to help him, with little to show. If only those back in the factory could see him now. We always regret what is possible, what is nearby. Coming to Vienna had been the right decision, it was either Vienna or Berlin, in Vienna the limitations of Europe as musical fortress were immediately apparent, his own limitations as well. "The piano is getting too narrow for me," was a line picked up by Delage, underlined. His straightforwardness, which may have been an advantage in the design and precision manufacture of a piano, left him in Vienna at a disadvantage. In a matter of days he saw himself as a more complex person, complexity, something he had not considered before, the complexities spreading from Amalia von Schalla, and her daughter, who was never far away, Elisabeth, his attraction to them, had in turn made him more complex, a man modified, just a little, which was enough; either that or he had never noticed or considered his complexities back at the home or at the factory, amongst people he could greet by name, putting up with his sister, she was different, she was his sister, his daily life in Sydney. The intricate situations in Vienna had become unavoidable, he had to take them into account, attractions were stronger than information or the difficulties of manufacturing or selling, Amalia seemed to be telling him, which in turn made him a more complex person. Not a cloud, and the green-blue sea glittering, the trails of white forming across the water, more or less parallel to one another, before dissolving. And the great depth of the ocean, always apparent. The ship continued pushing across the surface, a path of creamy-white in its wake, which was almost immediately erased, leaving no sign—an easy mockery of the ship's mighty engines and propellers. The sun on the small deck was bright enough for Delage to put on his sunglasses, the pale Dutchman in floppy khaki shorts squinted without, hardly anyone on the streets of Europe wore sunglasses, at least not in Vienna, Delage had noticed, in Sydney on the streets, even in the depths of winter, hardly a person was without their sunglasses. "I have loved maps," the Dutchman said. "'Loved' itself is a nuisance word. It is not a comfortable word. Nobody uses it with comfort. I can say I have loved looking at maps more than I loved looking at my wife. The fine lines and names on maps, most of all charts, where the fathoms are indicated with figures and colors, make you pleased to be human." Delage leaned over the rail listening to the pale Dutchman, the Englishman behind managed to secure his green seat in the sun, unconcerned his face was turning red, his wife had a floral towel over her head. The sisters had a habit of arriving late. It added to their invalid quality, everybody made way for them. The melancholy of the forsaken sister was having a stooping effect on the younger, attentive sister who had never married, and had not the slightest interest in marriage, she never thought about it, it never crossed her mind, not anymore, she told Elisabeth, I prefer being alone, she said more than once, the thought of living with somebody and taking their needs into account, it was altogether too difficult, aside from being unnecessary, she was happy with her own company and of other similar women, the 1930s apartment building in Elwood, Melbourne, where she lived had many single women, they did things together, such as having a coffee or small dinner parties, going to concerts, pottery classes. "Is she serious thinking that—I mean, about men?" Delage asked. "If it makes her feel better, then it is alright," said Elisabeth, who took little interest in other women. The attentive sister seemed to be a contented woman, she arranged her loyalties, looking after her disconsolate sister, more contented than the Englishwoman whose head was covered in a towel, who often appeared to be smiling to herself, alongside her husband, at the same time completely ignoring her husband, letting him get sunburned, they had become too familiar with one another. Now the sisters faced the sun, closing their eyes, allowing the warmth to soften their thoughts, the older, forsaken one undoing the top buttons of her blouse to extend the tan, after first rubbing cream into her feet and throat, the buttons on Amalia's pleated, high-collar blouse he found to be imitation buttons, decoration only, on her back well-hidden by the Italian pleating, which gave the impression of vertical stripes, was a tiny zipper of unexpected elegance. For Elisabeth, it was too hot on the small deck, she went back to the cabin, favoring an Austrian complexion over acquiring a tan, Delage remaining at the rail with the Dutchman. "Tell me something we don't already know," said the Englishman from under his hat, his eyes closed. "Where I grew up in South Australia, the houses had corrugated iron roofs," Delage said, when nobody else said anything. "And ours was the same red as this, on the deck here." "I love an iron roof on a house. I wish I grew up with an iron roof," the older sister spoke for the first time. "Especially when it rains," she went on, which made them all look at her. “There are no flies on a moving ship,” the Englishman observed, who could not imagine a corrugated iron roof, or why anyone would want to live under one, a factory or a warehouse, yes, not on a house, his eyes closed. “In Holland the thatch continues to flourish, I believe.” The *Romance* never stopped moving, day and night going forward, the steady vibration of the engines underfoot, so much distance to cover, so much deep water in the world, it was a wonder there could be any danger to rainfall or fish stocks, according to the captain. An albatross had landed on top of a container. In the morning it was still there, large, clumsy, on the following day too. Every effort was made to save the great bird. It was all they could talk about. The captain slowed the ship, still it couldn’t take off. On the small deck they gathered, Elisabeth too, the Dutchman taking the closest interest. “Of course, the albatross mustn’t die on a ship.” One of the crew had the idea of crawling out, wearing industrial gloves. All watched as he reached it, there was a struggle, the bird was struggling and snapping at his face and arms. “Careful,” the Dutchman said. The man got to his feet and threw the big bird up in the air—it dipped, working its wings, before flying off. The steel ship was warm to touch, in places hot. With nothing else available beyond the ship, only ocean, they lost the use of days, Thursday, Saturday, Monday, it hardly mattered, the feeling was one of being transported. By the fourth week they were well down the western side of Australia, although no sign of land, only iron-ore carriers going in the other direction, Delage increasingly wondered how Elisabeth would react to the place, all the more difficult for it being far away. Before she woke, Delage was up and making his way down the many layers of steps, almost to the waterline, where he could walk along the edge of the ship, a gangway with rail, holding on to the rail, the beginning of another day, the air cold, the empty ocean was like the day itself, one hundred and seventy paces, by his count, to where it (thick steel) tapered into the bow. Some mornings Delage went along and back twice. At this very end or front of the moving ship there was no wind, or sight of water, it was still, a neutral zone. Introducing his piano to Europe had not been a waste of time, or a difficult financial loss, on the contrary, something had come out of it, nothing is ever wasted, not entirely. It had left Delage an altered person, he was faintly aware, the normal version of himself was modified by his short time in Vienna, by Amalia, her daughter now on the ship, his reactions to them, separately and together, the reception of his piano, each had their effect on him; Konrad von Schalla too had been an influence. By the time he had left or fled Vienna, he was a modified person. The Dutchman had been drawn to the silent bow of the ship, more and more he sat there alone, thick chains and lines coiled nearby, as if he was smoking, only he wasn't smoking. Sometimes he didn't see Delage, which suggested he wanted to be left alone. The Dutchman didn't believe a grown person could change very much—only at small doses at the edges, hard to detect, especially to the person themselves. "I would go for a walk with you along the length of the ship, if there was room. If we were in the country we would walk, and I would talk. There would be the birds—sounds of birds. And don't they sound better than piano music? When we step ashore, you and I will go for our walk." Delage couldn't recall ever going on a long walk with a man, conversing over a range of subjects as they strode out, pointing with a gnarled stick to a flower or a butterfly, the Australian countryside actively discouraged walking of any kind, except as an endurance test, the example set by the early explorers who mostly died of thirst or exhaustion, some were speared, the difficulty being the heat, also the insects, the drooping khaki trees and bushes hardly help, above all the absence of paths and the reassurance of a distant spire. Europe is crisscrossed with meandering paths equipped with gates, stiles and signage for the convenience of walkers, it is impossible to go behind a bush in England without being disturbed by a walker or a pair of walkers, wearing stout tan shoes, in rude good health, taking up a path, as if they owned the land. In the von Schalla limousine, Elisabeth took him to the outskirts of Vienna, not far from the city center, where it became immediately rural, dense green, only a distant cement or chemical plant disturbing the scene, dark trees, small rivers. "Austria is not all 'heavy brick,' as you like to say," Elisabeth said, in a picnic voice. "Look, there's a cow!"—Delage joining in. But he wondered why he was there, he should be selling the virtues of his piano, it had become urgent to make some headway with his piano in Europe, even if he no longer knew where to turn, his chances increasingly looking slim. Having missed the *Romance* in Hamburg, he somehow had to catch it at La Spezia later in the week. "Our mother has invited a young composer tonight. She has arranged it for you." "Does she want me there?" Elisabeth looked at him, her mother was renowned for helping artistic people, but this man could not be called artistic, he was separate, from another place. While they sat on a rug near a tree, the chauffeur wandered off to smoke a cigarette, she opened a cardboard box of small savories; she had chocolates and held up an apple for each. Afterwards, Amalia lay with her head on his lap, he felt it necessary to rest his hand on her head, to hold it with its blond hair in place, she had closed her eyes, allowing him to look down on her face. Even when closed, her eyes appeared wide apart, quite a broad forehead. By hardly moving, though keeping a faint smile, she encouraged him to notice the rest of her body, the shape he could make out or begin to imagine beneath her dress; Delage became patient, with weak sun in his eyes, a picnic scene out of any number of French films, when he should have been working, instead of doing nothing but sitting with a woman and wondering what there was about him that could be of interest to her, Elisabeth, only daughter of the von Schallas, Austrian, a question so elusive he left it, it is always easier to draw a blank. Never had he thought so much about himself, a subject he generally touched upon before avoiding. She was eight or ten years younger than him, at least. "Mother's chosen composer might suit the sound of your piano," came her voice, eyes still closed. "Remember our critic suggested that? My mother makes situations into projects." Elisabeth sighed and did something her mother had done, she took his hand, placed it on her breast, rounder than he expected, young, alive. "I only have a few days left. I have to get down to business re my piano." She wasn't listening. "I can help you." "I don't think so. This piano is a technical object. You need to know what makes it different inside." At this Elisabeth sat up, which released his hand, the one with the watch on it pointing to the time. "It does not matter how it works inside. It is the sound that matters—the pleasure it gives." To show agreement, he touched her chin. The chauffeur had his hands in his pockets, looking the other way. "He's one of my mother's rescues," Elisabeth whispered in the car. He had played principal trumpet at the Vienna Philharmonic, but a few years ago had been caught in an avalanche while cross-country skiing, a pastime which strengthened his lungs for the trumpet playing, just about everybody in Austria has been caught in an avalanche, but he was buried for twenty minutes in this one, he was lucky to be found at all, let alone alive, pulled out purple with his mouth filled with snow, he could barely puff on a cigarette now, blowing a trumpet was out of the question, Delage could hear the labored breathing from the back, occasionally he glimpsed his mournful mustache. "It is not as if my mother likes the trumpet. It is not contemplative enough for her. It is the sort of instrument your father would play, she said to me." "A good woman," said Delage, who hardly knew her. "Do you think so?" her daughter replied. Delage had not heard of an avalanche ever taking place in Australia. They had driven further into the green countryside, Delage relaxed with her, Elisabeth, along the narrow roads, exceptionally neat villages, cleanliness seen as a force for conformity, always the church spire, they approached Vienna in a wide circle, and entered at a different point from where they had started. "I'm going to stand under a shower, and work out what to do with my life." What had been meant as mildly humorous, even if it did contain deadpan questions of hope, Elisabeth took seriously. She moved to reassure him. "Your life is full of interest! You have plenty ahead. And you have your health." At such unexpected optimism he gave one of his snort-laughs, which suggested above all affection. "Afterwards, we might have one of your so-called coffees, or something stronger." Frank Delage had an alert, shining quality, never downcast, there was always hope; it was what people found appealing in him. And Elisabeth had made him chirpy. She didn't have a career, she had no commercial or artistic ambitions. She was free. In the hotel he took off his clothes, and stood under the shower, as promised, soap in his eyes, and went over the possibilities. If the composer at dinner took no interest in the Delage piano, he'd finish with Vienna, explaining it to Amalia, and Elisabeth, it was time to go. There was no alternative. "I'm not here to enjoy myself." When he opened his eyes, he saw in the steam Elisabeth in her short dress, seated on the edge of the bath, watching him. "I've always wanted to do this." With the large towel she set about drying him, his shoulders, back and stomach, down to his knees, returning to his hair, all of which Delage allowed. Amalia herself opened the door expecting the contemporary composer, who had been recommended, she had only met him once or twice, in everyday life his timing was as random as his compositions, either he would arrive early or late, never on time, usually late, making an entrance with a kind of psychological crescendo long after everybody else had arrived and was waiting, the entrance of the soloist, not always dressed properly for the occasion, the hostesses were constantly put off-balance, but as a young composer it was allowed, artists too could arrive late in paint-splattered boots and trousers, the artist and composer can walk on water across most of Europe, when, opening the door Amalia saw, instead of the composer, her daughter with Delage, she looked from one to the other and saw the familiarity between them, helped by the two espressos at the nearby Schwarzenberg, Delage touching her arm as they went past. "At least somebody is here on time," she said to her husband in the small dining room. Another hour passed before the contemporary composer Paul Hildebrand arrived, by which time they were seated and eating. "We're not waiting for him any longer," von Schalla had said. In business, punctuality was assumed. "The artist has the fond feeling they have privileges. Where does that come from? In any other field, their behavior would be regarded as infantile." It allowed Delage to talk to him, always talk cautiously to a businessman, they're not partial to exaggeration, avoiding Amalia's indifference, she seemed distracted, the lateness of the contemporary composer had not been helpful, the evening had been arranged for the sole benefit of Delage, this visitor from Sydney, he was looking at her while talking to her husband. The composer Paul Hildebrand turned out to be tall, wearing a three-piece, pale-blue suit, and a necktie showing ferns, although there was not a single fern in all of Austria. He had combed-back hair, similar to Franz Liszt in the well-known photograph, the one with his cheek leaning against his hand, or rather, the tips of his fingers. Hildebrand was aware of his presence, he used it to promote his gifts. Certain authors (for example) disguise their self-absorption by perfecting in speech and dress an ostentatious modesty, others practice an extreme attentiveness. Both can be seen at book signings, writers' festivals, and in interviews, or when they're approached by strangers on the street. People meeting Hildebrand had no idea he was pathologically unpunctual. "No doubt you have already eaten, Mr. Hildebrand," von Schalla wiping his lips with the napkin. "And this is excellent beef." But Hildebrand who had not eaten was another elongated man who had a large appetite. "What sort of music do you write?" von Schalla went on, "I don't believe I have heard any." "The sound made by instruments—it's artificial. I add natural sounds. I also put silence to work. I make performance." Von Schalla nodded, his wife looking on. With his knife, he pointed, "Richard Strauss ate at this table holding the fork you have there in your hand." Hildebrand looked down at it. "*Ach!*" He threw it down, Strauss' fork, it bounced off the plate, splashing stroganoff over the front of his three-piece suit, quite a performance, for he continued eating the strips of beef and small onions using his fingers, leaving the fork on the floor. Delage had never seen anything like it, but then he had never met a contemporary composer before. "Richard Strauss was a very great composer. Behave yourself!" Amalia moved and sat next to him. "Mr. Delage here has come a long way. He is from Australia. He has designed and built a new piano. It has a wonderful new sound you might be interested in. I am bringing you together—two gifted men." Hildebrand had an impassive face, but managed to give Delage a cold glance, he had finished eating, said nothing to Delage or Amalia, waiting instead for the cheeses or the cognac, the way a concert pianist stares at the keyboard or up at the ceiling before beginning to play. "At least listen to what he has to say," she touched his arm. Von Schalla gave a pessimistic cough and stood up from the table, down in the Southern Hemisphere his only daughter was certainly old enough to do whatever she wanted, she was trying to shave Delage, against his protests, after a brief struggle at the mirror she had snatched his brush and razor, because she wanted to, she especially enjoyed carefully applying the lather, her playful actions made her appear younger, a sign of happiness also. And yet when he seized the shaving brush and went to lather her chin, Elisabeth put her hands up, cried out and shook her head, a slap of lather would make her into a bearded woman. Returning to her calm manner, she stood beside him as he finished shaving, pointing to the bits he had missed, made difficult by the bumping of the ship. Delage rinsed the brush. More than once his sister on the phone from Brisbane said how she envied men, by pulling faces every day shaving, their faces didn't age so rapidly, she'd picked it up in one of the magazines she flipped through, information Delage had been on the verge of sharing with Elisabeth, as he shaved, but decided against. Elisabeth had few responsibilities, she could recline on the small deck or on Delage's bed, reading, or glancing about in an interested manner, a woman accustomed to leisure. Alone, she could dream herself into a mermaid state, an especially shapely one, patient, compliant, without the coldness and the slipperiness, on a ship that went on day after day, the voyage never-ending. It was something Delage did not have a hope of imagining. And she had time to consider him, his easygoing acceptance of their situation; and she wondered if there was more. She didn't mind Delage spending hours on the small deck with the Dutchman, where she noticed for much of the time they had their elbows on the rail, in the midst of the waves, without actually saying anything. When he returned she would be waiting. To be on board a ship with a foreign man, a minor manufacturer from Sydney, his description, she hardly knew him, leaving behind her own familiar country, family, faces, the many local architectural and agricultural details, for an unknown desolate country far away, it had the aura of being taken, just like piracy in the old times. The raider manages to escape with his plunder. At first the captive struggles—she wants to scratch his eyes out. She is horrified, at the same time aware of having been chosen. Before long she becomes attracted to him, apparently it was not uncommon, an attraction made stronger by the circumstances. A mixed marriage has an undertone of piracy, the woman taken from her usual surroundings, taken into the unknown. All that was missing with Delage was the black beard and the weapon. And he was almost tall, without a perspiring forehead. He sat beside Elisabeth. "What are you going to do with me when you arrive?" He looked thoughtful, not at all fierce. "I'm thinking of putting you in a glass case in Hyde Park, with the sign 'Madwoman from Vienna.' I haven't quite decided on the words. I'll probably need your date of birth." "I am serious!" She was about to stand, instead she looked at him closely. Deflecting a question came easily, it was second nature to him, although it made him appear careless, another careless man, she knew he was not, a deflector but not a careless man, she had seen him do it before, it was a matter of waiting and choosing a better time. At this stage, Elisabeth wanted to discuss the near future, what she could expect from the New World. Whenever they had their elbows on the rail on the small deck, the Dutchman spoke about his wife, Delage said, how he had not paid attention or enough attention, under the same roof but living in a parallel manner, the Dutchman said several times, "parallel manner," her face and changing body, or her posture as she went about doing things, or what they had once done together, appeared before him, whether he wanted to be reminded or not. Often he wondered what she would be doing at a precise moment. Now that he had removed himself from Amsterdam there was room for her in the small city. It would be like the blinds being raised in the house. She could breathe. He was unlikely to return to Amsterdam. "She would not want to see me there, or anywhere." After thirty-seven years she preferred not to think about him anymore, let alone see him, even at a distance. If someone mentioned his name, she didn't appreciate it. "Since my wife has left me I can remember some things in perfect detail," his elbows on the rail. There had been three birds sitting on the stern passing through the Malaccas, bigger than pigeons, and a smaller gray one fidgeted more than the others. Every afternoon the English couple were heard arguing, before appearing on the small deck as a neat, composed couple, as if nothing had happened. "In our time together, my wife and I never raised our voices," the Dutchman told Delage. He went on to say he was being saved by sensations, at regular and not so regular intervals he would see or hear something, an unexpected thought that didn't seem to relate to anything, a forgotten memory, there were speculations, a possibility might come forward, which managed to hold his attention at different times for hours on end. The world consisted of thoughts and reactions to thoughts.

Remember the difficulties of conversations, the inequality of them, each person is wanting to impress the other, slipping into a more attentive persona, hoping for the other to think well of them, the nodding and the quickly responding laugh, seeking approval, seeking agreement, cutting of the cloth, hoping to talk them around, the shifting of the other one's position, a conversation can never be neutral, stable, innocent. Frank Delage had the tendency to go quiet, or become over-accommodating, or else lose track or speak humorously, inevitably coming across as reckless or foolish, characteristics which can be attractive, but in business become an immediate disadvantage, in Europe especially. How could someone like him have designed and built in all its intricacy a concert grand in a choice of timbers—in Sydney, Australia? Delage tried to be carefree in conversation. By the fourth or fifth day in Vienna he retreated from talking, or talking earnestly, which was usually how he ended up talking about the Delage piano, the one subject he could handle with real authority. Of course in Vienna it was not possible to avoid conversations, he was forced to describe the workings of his piano to anyone who would listen, beginning with Amalia von Schalla on the footpath, elegant woman, all in the hope of converting someone, anyone, he could hear himself saying the same things and cluttering the sentences with factual information, how else to describe the advantages of his piano which were as clear as daylight to him, as a consequence Delage began talking more to himself, at the table or on the street, his lips moving. And yet Amalia and her daughter, Elisabeth, landlocked women, didn't seem to mind. After the cognac, von Schalla, who was talking about how artistic types were inept when it came to promoting themselves, suddenly stood up, the contemporary composer Hildebrand followed, Delage joined them, the two women remained seated at the table, a discarded mother and daughter, it happens, clamming up is in our family, Delage's sister reminded him when she didn't have anything else to say, Delage looked from one woman to the other, at least he made the effort, they each motioned him on. Down the hall, von Schalla unlocked the door to his room. "We can have our talk here." There was a desk, books in a glass cabinet, Persian carpets, heavy curtains. On the walls were women painted by Egon Schiele, naked and spread-eagled, as well as erotic studies by other artists, all kinds, not suitable for public viewing, prints by Utamaro, and cabinets of French postcards, mixed with American photographs, some of recognizable film stars completely naked.

Photographers can hardly be included as artists. It is truer to say that, having reduced the significance of art, photographers are the enemy of art. "My wife disapproves. She of course doesn't enjoy coming here. I consider it healthy." He poured them all another cognac. The composer remained studying the photographs. "I want you, over there, to listen. And you, kindly explain to our composer friend the merits of your piano. You did say it had advantages over the competing products?" Yes, he did. And in an almost offhand manner Delage listed them. Following the music critic's suggestion he emphasized the piano's new sound, some would say an austere, unforgiving sound. Such a sound could match the intolerant ambitions of contemporary music, Delage repeated verbatim. Here von Schalla interrupted, and appeared to change the subject. "How many pianos do you make in a given year? And their cost to make is? How much do they sell for? Think about this. Pianos look all the same—or am I missing something? They're black." "They're not all black." He waved away Delage's objections. "Make yours different. Give it a name. What about your famous bird, the kookaburra? Have the bird big in gold leaf above the keyboard. It would become like the three-pointed star." Hildebrand had returned to examining the photographs, humming a tune as he went from one to the other, it could take all night and the next, there were dozens of naked women in different poses from different cultures, Hildebrand needed an event or a scene of some kind before he could even consider the first note, Beethoven took from the weather and pastures, or the life of an emperor, in Australia contemporary composers are always on the alert for subjects to illustrate, bushranger stories are a favorite source, and deserted settlements being overrun by nature, the melancholy of it, wherever possible imitating with strings the shimmering heat and sounds of insects. Von Schalla had to speak sharply to get Hildebrand back into the conversation. The master businessman was renowned for his quick movements in negotiations, it was what he did every day of the week. Bringing together the piano manufacturer and a local composer, although important to the visitor from Sydney, was by his standards a minor matter. He was doing it to keep his wife happy. And this Delage in his ill-fitting suit had probably saved his life. It was all about mutual benefit, von Schalla had pointed out. After listening without so much as a nod, unlike Delage, who realized he had been nodding too much, the composer agreed to give the Delage piano a hearing, Hildebrand, who Delage noticed was perspiring, said he would travel alone out to the warehouse, it would take only a few minutes to make a decision. "I will need to test the sound, I do not make use of just any sound," he smiled at von Schalla. Only then would he have it delivered to his studio at Pötzleinsdorf. It was agreed, all three were shaking their hands as Elisabeth walked in. Delage made a move to stop her, concerned with what she could not avoid seeing on the walls, but Elisabeth came over to him, her father and Hildebrand went on talking, obviously she knew of the existence of the collection; later she told Delage such collections were common in the nineteenth century, not only amongst the Hungarian and Austrian gentry, the English formed collections of erotica too, something you would not expect of them, or perhaps that's precisely what the English would be expected to do, Delage smiling at her free use of "connoisseur," and went on smiling at language in general. Her father's collection of erotica was one of the finest in private hands, connoisseurs from all over the world came to the house to see it, she said, her father enjoyed observing their excitement and envy; as she came forward, Delage without saying anything put on an expression of agreement. It was his first success in Europe, a beginning, it could well lead to something significant, it was now in the hands of the contemporary composer Hildebrand to compose something on the Delage piano. A pale-brownish line above the blue-green was the first sign of land, and birds came near the ship, the line barely visible remained solid against the liquid foreground, the English couple no longer argued, at least for a few days, the sisters from Melbourne joined the others at the rail, the German officers were more talkative too, there was a general lightheartedness on the ship, only the Dutchman seemed uninterested, turning his back on land. The surfaces of the *Romance* constantly felt unstable, the land ahead would be firm. The captain who had taken to speaking to Elisabeth in German said they would dock in Fremantle the following evening. Although there was no certainty the contemporary composer in the three-piece suit would take to the sound of his piano, Frank Delage nevertheless was grateful. The trip had not been entirely in vain. "Great oaks from little acorns grow." And without Amalia's interest, the possible association with the composer would not have happened, he wanted to thank her, she was waiting in her room, Elisabeth instead took him in the opposite direction, even though his thoughts were with Amalia waiting for him, he followed Elisabeth down the other end of the hall, antlers, ancestral clocks, portraits, weapons, Elisabeth leading him, to her room. She had a carefree manner, tossing her scarf which floated over an armchair. Elisabeth's room was just as spacious as her mother's. The scattered arrangement of impressions, as if the entire space was a collage, had an instinctive modernity, different from her mother's deliberate style. Delage recognized a Bechstein grand. Near it was a painting of overlapping American flags, further along a golden woman in a bath, by the door a drawing or a print of a rhinoceros—more objects and others for him to take into account. On the floor in an impatient pile were a few illustrated books. Delage lifted the lid of the piano. "It's out of tune." "I have not played for at least a year. I've lost interest." She stood near him. She had studied art history, and for that reason had lost interest in art as well. Universities have a horror of aesthetics, tutors can more readily discuss the political situation of the time, historical influences such as class or the discoveries in science, or the misfortunes of race and gender, which undoubtedly lie behind the brushstrokes of every painting, even if the painter was unaware of it, much easier for tutors and students to handle facts, people cling on to loose bits of timber during a shipwreck, avoid confusion, decisions on aesthetics being far more difficult than enumerating facts, impossible for some. "I've decided to concentrate more on persons. What do you think about that?" Looking up,

Elisabeth's face was pale in shadow, a face smoothed by candlelight. Delage began to wonder whether he should be alone with her. He had told her mother, Amalia, he wanted to see her in her room, she would be waiting for him. It is difficult to decide between what is nearby, and what is more obscurely outside, how to remain loyal to one, or to the other. And many thoughts he resisted, until slowly he came around. Sitting at the piano would take his mind off, or turn his thoughts back to his piano, not this one, beyond to Sydney, to the factory which made the new piano, everybody working there he knew by their first names, he made a point of greeting them whenever he walked through, a lighthearted one to the Slovakian bookkeeper, they were relying on him, entire families depended on his business acumen, whether or not he could sell even one Delage grand piano into Europe, now for the first time he could report he had made progress, began playing the Bechstein, as if that would solve anything. He was immediately repelled by its complacent old sound, as Elisabeth came and sat on him, legs apart, her back to the keyboard, Delage reduced to playing one hand, making mistakes, another, he was only playing scales on the Bechstein, more mistakes, deliberate wrong notes, comically, he was hoping, to suggest his incomprehension, Elisabeth had her hands around his neck, as Delage played louder, but tuneless, comically he hoped. It happened as they left the Mediterranean too, she hitched her skirt over him, as if he was hers. Through the Malaccas, past Sumatra, all through the Java Sea, sunsets became a performance, the fiery spread made them cry out. Clouds along the bottom of the sky became heat affected, bar-radiator red aglow, the Englishman exclaimed, recalling his digs in Clapham, the pink of lipsticks or cockatoos (puffy gray at the edges), while further south it was less humid, and clouds on the horizon took on a streaked honey yellow, shooting out glittering lines, such an immense statement of day ending, the heat-stained sky fading to blue-black, darkness, stars. Elisabeth had never experienced anything like it. In the Alps, sunset color would appear at the ends of valleys, which had snow on either side like stage curtains, but half-hidden, the sunsets diminished by the bulk of mountains, the peaks, and the mass of snow. If Elisabeth was late, Delage would rush down the steps and get her up for a viewing on the small deck. Nothing can be learned from a sunset, unless the colors exuberantly produced by nature throw into doubt notions of what is, or not, kitsch.

He had almost missed the *Romance* at La Spezia, the great black funnel had been smoking, the gangway was being winched up from the wharf, crew stood about fore and aft ready to release the lines, Delage arrived in a taxi, the driver sounding the horn mercilessly, the Italian instinct for melodrama, it drove fast along the wharf to the middle of the ship, and stopped. In fact, his entire time in Vienna had not followed a logical path, it had been hasty, improvised, irrational, either he was waiting or he was running late, unsure of what he should do next, realizing more confusion than what can be retained, it was a condensed version of his life in Sydney, how too many things happened without his intention, he needed support, a presence alongside, something his sister had been nudging him toward, not that her life was anything to go by, the door behind opened, Delage facing the piano couldn't turn his head. Elisabeth stirred, or adjusted on his lap. "My father. Was he looking for you?" Unhurried, she put on her clothes, "He should not burst in like that." With his hand near her neck, he felt her warmth. "I said I'd see your mother." It was not a matter of fleeing, there was no reason to feel awkward or confused, he was accustomed to women of Elisabeth's generation being at ease in this and other situations. "Disappointments lead to accusations," "It is necessary to be skeptical," "Why do the contraltos show rotten taste in blue sheath dresses?" these were thoughts that had caught Delage's eye; he'd forgotten where he'd come across the first two, the third was his own, hardly a thought at all, an observation, of little or no value he'd be the first to admit, at the few recitals where his piano was being used he couldn't believe his eyes. He liked to settle and be thoughtful, it was how one morning on a train he had visualized the new mechanical movements of the Delage piano. After Elisabeth's father had burst in on them, he felt positively lighthearted making his way to Amalia's room, anticipating her face, tilted manner, Elisabeth said she would be at his hotel at ten, brushing his arm as he went. Further along, the door opened and von Schalla came out of his room. "I was interested to have your opinion of my collection. And what did you make of our composer?" Lowering his voice, "You might consider returning to your hotel." "I wanted to say thanks to her—Amalia, I'm talking about." Delage's brevity was local, a national characteristic, it had no flow, it couldn't wander around a subject, finding the beneficial level. "I can convey your apologies. She'll understand. It's up to you, of course." "Are you quite sure about that?" Delage went on looking at von Schalla, who didn't bother answering. It could have been part of the general oldness of things, Vienna exerted such a feeling, people in heavy coats moving slowly, which was why he remained half-blocked by von Schalla in the long hall, over his shoulder he could see the door to Amalia's room where she was said to be waiting, the husband had not prevented him but advised against, enough for one night, his opinion, not standing in his way, only half-blocking. In the hall one of the light bulbs had blown. He wondered if von Schalla had noticed. After all, he was a man who never looked tired. Delage hesitated, he didn't know why. Pianos were not the only things that were complex. Still wide awake, he sat on the bed and thought of calling the factory, nine in the morning Sydney time, to see how they were going, he had nothing much to add to what they already knew. Alternatively, he could phone his sister, a thought he immediately dismissed. She would get into a flap at being called from Vienna, she would jump to the conclusion something had happened, an accident, he was stretched out struggling for breath in an unknown hospital—why else would he call? And it happened to be that Vienna stood at the very top of the places she wanted to visit, she had never been overseas, aside from New Zealand, more than ever she believed she could no longer travel alone, not to a distant country, even England, where there would be no problems with language, but the direction of streets, the small change and the weather would be unfamiliar, she had been suggesting to her brother they should take a holiday together, not to Bali or Thailand, or anywhere in Malaysia, not to a humid country, even though she lived in Brisbane, Queensland, a city with the worst humidity imaginable, in February virtually unlivable, such an inhospitable place encourages the short cut, informality, reminiscences of the most basic kind, where cashew nuts and peanuts are eaten by the handful before meals, it was Europe she had in mind, starting off with Vienna. Early each morning one of the crew used a high-pressure hose to remove salt from the small deck and other areas, something Delage and the Dutchman enjoyed watching, without saying a word. In Perth, when he did phone the factory, the Slovakian bookkeeper, who had taken to answering the phones, said his sister had been on the phone every other day for news of him, "warts and all," as she reported it. People trust each other on the slightest acquaintance. And so the small everyday movements of the world are allowed to continue. To have the future of the factory in the hands of a virtually unknown Viennese composer who wore an absurd blue suit, too light in color, just as Hildebrand's hair was too long for a lanky man, the three-piece suit and hair certainly missed the mark, the lanky composer nevertheless had barely acknowledged him, perhaps sensing a rival for Amalia von Schalla's well-known generosity; Delage intended to ask Amalia for her frank opinion of Hildebrand, when he thanked her for going to the trouble of securing the composer, except, after some hesitation, Delage had returned to his hotel. He was not sleeping well. Naturally he had concerns about his business. The cost of this trip exceeded the profit of an entire Delage grand piano. The strong ship was moving forward, the liquid surface resisted, fur resisting the crawl of an insect, still the ship advanced, the flat coastline of Australia disappearing, reappearing along one side. "The fresh air is doing her the world of good," the Melbourne sister reported. "Her appetite has returned. My sister is a natural cook. You should see her kitchen—the copper pans, the table settings. Men are always leaving women who are brilliant cooks, as well as women who are not cooks, who, in fact, don't like cooking at all. I don't think they know what they want. How long is it you two have been together?" On the small deck, Elisabeth often found herself caught with one of the sisters, or both, which she didn't mind, the situation between sisters she found endlessly interesting. To Delage's surprise, she had never shown sympathy for the older, discarded sister who enjoyed the cooking. Whenever he returned from being somewhere on the ship with the Dutchman, Elisabeth wanted to hear what they had been talking about, or rather, what the Dutchman had to say, he doing most of the talking. The days were clear and hot, they hardly varied. Some days Delage answered, "Nothing. We didn't say a word." Elisabeth threw her arms up to the sky, "You spend hours together, and you say nothing?" "I was waiting for him to say something, he was waiting for me. Yesterday a seagull shat on his head. He said it was bad luck—what most other people would call 'auspicious.'" Soon afterward the Dutchman said he had heard through a "third party" his wife, or ex-wife, was no longer in Europe, but in Perth, staying with a friend she had first met at a poetry festival. "In the 1970s, her friend was crossing a bridge in Amsterdam and collided with an Australian tourist, a garage-door salesman, and fell off her bicycle—and followed him to the Great South Land. The marriage didn't last. She stayed on in Perth because of the children. How would she get along there? When I met her, she had on an apron-dress like a milkmaid, normally seen only in Switzerland. I don't think she ever approved of me. You can imagine what they would have been talking about." Delage wondered whether it was a good idea meeting her. "My wife knew I was on the ship. It looks to me as if she wants to come back. I'll see her. Of course I will. I'm going to have to choose my words carefully." As they approached Fremantle, the Dutchman was out on the small deck early, where he stayed all day, Delage pointed to the dangers of sunstroke, he would not have experienced such a sun in Europe, it was a matter of wearing a hat at all times, however the Dutchman waved away the advice, he held on to the rail and breathed in deeply, a land with a clear optimistic smell, according to his nostrils. It is the future, I like it, he said several times. Apparently he could smell the red soil, dust and dry grass of Western Australia, which was visible on the horizon only through binoculars. "Leaving a wife is like a killing," he went on to tell Delage. "Usually it is not deserved. By any measure it is not a good feeling. A marriage," he said to Delage, "should never be based on one subject." Delage waited for Elisabeth's reaction. "If you remember," Elisabeth in their cabin, "it was she who left him. Or am I mistaken here?" "It's probably complicated," Delage said. "There are many things we don't know. He has become cheerful, which has to be good." Whenever she touched his cheek and smiled, he knew she was allowing a lack of understanding. They were encircled by shared aspects of themselves, a short radius, "radius" an attractive word, a contemplative word, "a tad," "robust" (as in "discussion"), and "clam chowder," all ridiculous words, not as contemplative as the wonderful "radius," the English-speaking world and the world in general would be better off without them. "Grinned" and "grinning" could also go. Ever since her visit to the hotel at ten the following morning, Elisabeth was liquid, warm, all attention. From ten in the morning until the following day they had stayed in his room, Elisabeth's surrendering softness had given Delage experience of Amalia, Elisabeth having aspects of her mother, being part of her and grown beyond, landlocked women, Elisabeth too had an oblique manner, she also accepted the world around her as hers—her way of looking down, or sideways at others, or not looking at all. Delage could see the effect of his personality, when normally he couldn't. They, Elisabeth, her mother, Amalia von Schalla, had not been the reason for traveling to Vienna, he had never heard of them before, had not known of the existence of the Schalla family, there were obviously many people or situations like them, a particular mother and daughter, in Europe especially; they were occupying more of his thoughts than the piano, Elisabeth in particular, her clothes tangled amongst his shirt, dark trousers and socks on the floor, his thoughts, and her mother three streets from the hotel, if that, waiting at attractive arm's length in a room, a woman who always appeared to be waiting, not a café- or a parks-and-garden-woman, a room-woman, waiting in a room, her own. As the significance or the mystery of it unfolded, the problems presented by the perpetual piano, which had filled his mind leaving space for little else, the more he thought about it the less he actually thought about it, receded. Unannounced, Amalia von Schalla was at the door. "You are here? Thank you very much." She was wearing a small spinach-colored hat and veil, not for her daughter. "Tell him I wish to speak to him. Preferably now. If not, tonight." "He has to rush off tomorrow to catch a boat." "Tell him, if you wouldn't mind." Delage was drying his hair. "What was all that about?" "Nothing really," Elisabeth said. Generally speaking, by the way, actually, as a matter of fact, these could be banished, or at least their usage reduced, along with meanwhile, back at the ranch. Observations about the weather, the enunciation of past, present, future temperatures, a specialty of uncertain women, could go the way of thus, see you anon. These automatic weather concerns have little meaning, other than acting as conversation fillers. "Looks like rain"—what does that mean? Konrad von Schalla was a man not known for taking an interest in the weather, good or bad, it was all the same to him, a matter of getting the clothing right, especially the shoes, that was all. It became one less thing to think about. The one time he almost said something about the weather was to lump the unreliability of economic forecasters in with the equally hapless weather forecasters. If he had listened to the so-called experts in the economic forecasting business he would have fallen by the wayside years ago, he said to Delage. As if to challenge von Schalla's indifference, Delage was caught out in a downpour in the middle of Opernring on his way to the Schallas' apartments on Argentinierstrasse. He arrived drying his face with a handkerchief, the bottom half of his trousers and shoes saturated. "Vienna is full of surprises," he intended to open with, unaware of von Schalla's horror of even the most innocent reference to weather, it was Amalia, Elisabeth's mother, he had come to see, he should have gone to her room the night before (or the night before that?), even now he should have gone first to her, instead he was following von Schalla to the larger of the rooms, which served as his office. Facing him across the small desk, Delage saw again his extreme neatness. Every woven fiber in his English suit, shirt and tie was pressed into service, his small black shoes buffed, hair combed, trimmed nails, small patient hands. The neatness drew attention to itself. Delage kept noting the details of it, a neatness which kept him and anybody else at a manageable distance, the way extreme neatness of dress is put forward as a standard by pontiffs, the British royal family, army officers. Seated at his undersize desk he spoke without taking his eyes from Delage, one or two of his fingers moving slightly. "There is so much ordinariness in the world, I am surprised there is not more irritation, even in private. I do not see how anybody with ambitions can be pleased with what is around them. Wherever you look there is something to correct possible optimism. The great majority of men and women are satisfied merely to get by, they don't mind being ordinary," he said. "It is the majority that makes the cities and towns ugly, a small minority keeps trying to raise the level. The creators and the destroyers. I think it is something we can agree on," he gave a short smile. "It is the same story in every society, every country, the same situation—the weight of the majority brings with it a lowering. No doubt more in your Australia, it being new. I am told things are very plain there—otherwise, what are you doing here?" Everybody in Europe had an opinion or a disappointment. The disappointment led to the other. Most of von Schalla's complaints were familiar, which allowed Delage to nod a little, enough, the moment they became unreasonable he turned to Elisabeth, naked, waiting at the hotel, the daughter of this man holding forth across. And what a luxury that was. "Then there are the women, our wives and our daughters, who have become restless. They require distractions, moving about, they never stay in the one spot. They are free to do anything now, and it is encouraged by the modern transport system. The clothes they wear are designed for moving freely." Elisabeth arrived at the hotel in khaki trousers, a quilted jacket, flat ochre-red shoes with blue laces. "If my wife is not attending a concert, she is at the theater, if not the theater she is at a public lecture of some kind—usually a subject she has not until then shown an interest in. The theater world, and I include the music world, those opinionated people flapping about on stage, pulling faces, shouting, or looking mournful. They beg us to look at them. As if we need to be entertained. At least my daughter seeks her entertainments elsewhere." Delage glanced at his watch. He began to move. "Only a fool would get it into their head to begin over again, and remanufacture an instrument that has already been manufactured, centuries ago, then expect Europe, which is stuffed full of pianos, where the piano was invented, to welcome your new piano with wide-open arms. I am sorry, it is not possible. At the same time," using his harsh voice, "it is impressive. I would have to say, yes." Already Delage had been thinking how to report the conversation to Elisabeth, she would want to hear every bit of it, including nuances, in turn she would be amazed at his meandering and missed detail, he could never recall a conversation properly, unlike his sister, who had an unshakable memory when it came to it, Elisabeth too, he had not failed to notice, was strong on conversational details. "And there is always the temptation to let it all slip," von Schalla had said, "become one with the sloppy plumber, the house painter leaving the mess, the second-rate architect, God knows there are too many of them, the pianist who misses the notes. The list goes on. Or you can stay above." Delage was no longer sure where he stood, what he had achieved. He wasn't sure whether it was necessary to say anything. "I would have liked you to see my piano. Even if you are not musical." "Who told you that?" von Schalla said sharply. Then gave a discreet cough, "Good luck with your endeavors. I don't know what more we can do." "'Endeavors.' There's a word you don't hear anymore. You've been kind to me—hospitable. I would like to thank you," shaking hands. And he meant it, one part of his life completed, as he went down the corridor to Amalia von Schalla's room, where she stood in the middle of the room, almost as tall as he was, made taller by what was a hostess gown, a long gray coat, large buttons. "I was waylaid by your husband. I am leaving in the morning." "Then it was nice of you to call. I feel privileged." She turned away. "I do have something to tell you. In your absence the composer has agreed to make use of your piano. It has been delivered. He sees possibilities, he said, although the color makes him sick." "Thank you." "You have a courageous piano," she said loudly, "but you do not know how to behave." "'A courageous piano?'" Delage snorted happily at the English. Amalia swung around, "What have I done to you? Why are you doing this?" Delage took a step forward, wary of the slap. "I should have come here last night," he touched her elbow. "I am sorry. I should have. I wanted to. And I have to go tomorrow." He tugged at her coat, which opened. Wherever possible, Amalia von Schalla converted her dissatisfactions into musical appreciation, and other creative endeavors. Music softened her. And she saw how her name, money and recommendations made a difference, Vienna had the normal population of desperately seeking artists and fragile performers, most she kept at a distance, she had happened upon Frank Delage in the music shop and listened to him outside on the street. He was saying, "First, I have to get to La Spezia. I have to get there in a hurry." It was a geographical way of expressing regret, in a roundabout way acknowledging her presence, if she would allow it, but either it had missed the mark or she was somewhere else, her face had tilted away then up, she was abrupt, and he was conscious of her daughter, Elisabeth, her shadowy whiteness enormous above him, her easy way of talking. Her mother was not easy, she had assumed a confused coldness. "After he listened to your piano, the composer agreed it had a fresh sound. Already an idea has come to him, Hildebrand said. He'll be doing it quickly. I hope our efforts have you satisfied." She went on to say a small concert hall that promoted contemporary works had already been booked. "You could perhaps stay for it. I am sure you can find plenty in Vienna to occupy yourself." She looked at him. "Perhaps you are not interested, now that you have what you wanted." Without waiting, she said in a strange voice, "I am my daughter." If Delage had been about to say something, he stopped. Still facing him, she bared a breast, and held it for him, almost an offering, he couldn't be certain, her face had turned gaunt, high-cheek beauty, at a glance Delage saw nothing there of her daughter, unless the eyes and cheeks. The room was insistently modern, the breast put forward didn't seem out of place, on the contrary, the clean furniture, bold colors, paintings and photographs encouraged such a live presentation. Delage was unable to decide what to do, what was required, if anything was required, in the morning early he was leaving Vienna. It was not possible to stay, it would be difficult to leave. "What I am thinking—" "Please go." Without moving, she kept her breast bare, its shape filling her hand. "I think you should go now." Decisiveness, the ability to think on your feet, blind faith, personal hygiene, volubility were just a few of the requirements for a successful piano manufacturer, especially one operating from a political, industrial and musical outpost, Sydney, anybody on the factory floor would vouch for F. D.

having each of these qualities, plus a few more, optimism, stamina, irritability, although his sister and the Slovakian bookkeeper were more realistic. Qualities which had been necessary for a piano manufacturer were not necessarily useful in everyday life. For at least twenty seconds Delage stood, unsure what to say, words which would express more than gratitude, it was not something she was interested in, she existed above gratitude, at least an appreciation of her beauty, her face and hands, her perfect breast still exposed, praise he had withheld when he should have given it, but could hardly now, from the moment they met she had held his interest, he could have told her that, he had no idea who she was then, without her presence Vienna would have been a cold, difficult place. If it had been Berlin, this could not have happened. It was through Amalia von Schalla he was allowed into the Schalla house, and so he entered Europe, their daughter waiting back at the hotel. Of all people he didn't want to disappoint Amalia, let alone make her unhappy, although there was little chance of that. Lack of consideration could well have appeared as lack of interest, it was never meant, a possibility nevertheless, moving to the door while twisting the top half of his body toward her, she in the middle of the room, at the door Delage paused, and once in the hall stood outside the door, one hand on the handle, how he was left feeling, and obviously looked, foolish. It was a retreat, it could only be temporary. A retreat was unnecessary. He was about to reenter, she could well have been waiting, expecting him, it would not be surprising, although it still may not have been what she wanted, not at all, his hand went forward, knuckles raised to knock. From along the corridor a voice called out, "Before you are leaving, I have something further to say." Different people fit differently in different rooms. The Schalla apartments were large and high-ceilinged, the corridor as interminable as any Delage had come across, anywhere, the large rooms and the corridor dwarfed von Schalla, already a short figure, who nevertheless moved about in the large spaces with ease, as if he belonged to them, his wife, Amalia, restless, uncomfortable, different. Von Schalla was coming toward him—meeting him halfway. "I don't know if my wife has told you, I have bought the piano for her." He was looking carefully at Delage. "My wife seemed very pleased when I told her. Who knows what she'll do with it. It has a rarity value. There cannot be many examples of the Delage piano in Europe. She could build a museum around it?" This was sudden, too sudden, not at all what he, Delage, wanted. It had been done without his knowledge, behind his back, as it were, for a reason, unless both von Schalla and Amalia wanted to surprise him. He couldn't imagine them working together. Delage managed to say, "No," which von Schalla ignored. "As far as I am concerned, it is money well spent. I spoke to your factory, a woman, young by her voice. Who said she came from our part of the world? Very nice, I would say an attractive woman. Every sale was more than welcome, she said to me. She was very clear. Your factory is running short of cash. You are not in a strong position. Or don't you know your own situation?" The *Romance* docked at night, the bright lights seen from a distance, Fremantle, gray-white concrete closer and primary colors stacked in rows, the ship approached almost silently, figures here and there, a car drove along the wharf parallel, its windows glittering, the illuminated wharf forming a vast semicircle of light fading into darkness beyond. Elisabeth leaned against Delage at the rail. "This is what I have gone across the world for?" "This is it," Delage made a grand gesture. "Wait until the sun comes up." The salt was hosed off the decks and rails, only to accumulate again by the next morning, sharp enough to leave tiny cuts on Elisabeth's hands. Earlier, she had said, "My parents do not know I am here. On a boat going to Australia is the last place they would consider." What? "I do not tell them where I am every minute." South of Singapore, she whispered in his ear, "If you are a piano manufacturer, you must be very conservative." After a quick breakfast, the Dutchman was the first to step onto Australia, the land he had heard so much about, here it was oil-stained reinforced concrete, "*Terra firma*," he waved back at the others. He was setting forth, aiming for the first available barber shop, more of a waddle than an anticipatory walk, a dumpy rolling figure in sandals with Continental black socks, and holding in a paper bag the books he had finished on the voyage, true to self being absolutely essential when meeting a former wife, or the one previous, they look to console themselves by observing the worst characteristics displayed again by the man they had foolishly wasted valuable years on. There was a warm land breeze, something the English couple had never experienced before. Lifting their suitcases down the gangway, they already were arguing about the weather, a pointless argument, if ever there was, although necessary to them, she was sick to death of his certainties, she told him, not in a whisper, a hiss-shout, everybody could hear, their irritability made worse by the flies. "What sort of country is it that allows this many flies?" The sisters from Melbourne drew back from venturing into Fremantle, let alone Perth half an hour to the north, they retreated to their cabin, and remained there for the short duration. Now that they were back in their own country, the fact of their situation lay before them without distractions, a time of difficulties, of adjustment, surrounded by what was familiar. Sailors look forward to land, and immediately want to go back to sea. From the container wharf to the city center, the streets were typical of those found around ports and airports, many long sheds, service roads, trucks in line, gray tones, not many women, the center of Fremantle, which radiated from the harbor, blue-green glitter mixing it with clusters of swaying masts and red brick, Delage and Elisabeth reached by taxi. It was not long before they stopped walking, and sat outside for a coffee by the harbor. "Everybody has excellent teeth," Elisabeth observed. Delage looked up from the newspaper. "It's just everybody smiling." "It does look happy and amazingly healthy," Elisabeth said, although she didn't look happy at all, a worried look he hadn't seen before, Delage considered also the choices being made by the Dutchman, and wondered whether the extra sympathy he felt was a result of age. The ship was sailing in the evening. They drove through sand, past red- and gray-tiled houses, awnings and blinds fitted over the windows, all suburbs were hot, where bushes strove to reach knee high, one suburb in there called Hopeland, another Success. New suburbs attract the most appalling names in Australia. A suburb could hardly be called Failure, no one would want to bring up children there, in Methodist Adelaide they have Paradise, as if anyone would want to live in Purgatory or Hell—but why would Perth's town-planners come up with Success? New settlements on the fringe of bare continents appear as scratches on the surface, tentative, self-conscious, ever hopeful. Signs of sand everywhere in Perth. Elisabeth and Delage wandered about, there was simply nothing to see, certainly not on foot, the hot-looking eucalypts, reflections and space. The Delage concert grand had a greater presence in Vienna than in Perth, Delage said to Elisabeth, who was subdued. There was not a single Delage piano in all of Western Australia, which was far bigger than Germany, France, Portugal and Austria combined, he pointed out. Elisabeth patted his hand to indicate understanding. The attractions of Perth were hidden, centered on family, even more than in most cities. The captain had told Elisabeth the containers unloaded were filled with tennis rackets, footballs, cricket bats, sunglasses, Italian bicycles, punching bags, Chinese beach umbrellas.

"She didn't want to see me at all, it was a serious misreading on my part. I have never heard her speak loudly, it was because she was at her friend's house. She asked what was I doing here. You have ruined everything, and now you come here, she pointed at me. Who do you think you are? There was no need for us to speak again. Spoke to me in that way. I didn't know what to say. I handed her the books, she may have been interested. She threw them to one side without looking at them. Then she began to cry. I thought I should at least touch her on the shoulder, to be of assistance, but thought better of it. Her friend from Amsterdam in her little apron-dress stood up and asked me to leave. On the path to the gate, her twelve-year-old son began throwing gravel at me. At the gate I met the garage-door salesman, come to visit the children. He saw in an instant what was happening. He talked to me about garage doors. The business was booming, he said to me. Home-owners in Perth and Fremantle wanted not one but two or three garages, each with the tilting or roll-up door, his firm could supply either. A lot of houses here have two cars, or one car plus the boat, he explained, or two cars and boat. And these need protection from the elements, he said. He could not keep up with the demand for garage doors. He quoted figures. It made him cheerful. He was a cheerful and energetic man, I saw he was the opposite to me. He had no doubts. I explained I was from Holland, and did not possess a garage, but he gave me his card." High waves came in twos and threes, the ship had to point into them, the famed Southern Ocean, sending up spray which came down heavier than rain all over the ship. "It is an advantage to be pleased with the sound of your voice," von Schalla behind his desk. "Everybody is aware of his own voice. As you talk, you listen to your own voice, make adjustments to it as you speak, listening to your own opinions, your choice of words, loud or soft, and approve of them. If you do not listen to your voice," he said in Vienna, "you will not attract buyers to your piano. And never be concerned about repeating yourself." For the first few days, Delage spent as much time as possible with the Dutchman, who couldn't stop talking, in all their time together on the small deck he had never heard the Dutchman talk as much, they were in the Southern Ocean, he was going over the same thing again and again, the ship met the procession of long gray waves, one followed by another, another, again, the Dutchman was incapable of changing the subject, which was his wife or former wife, he had a moist swallowing action Delage hadn't noticed before, his tongue darted forward which showed bewilderment, the influence of the woman she had become friends with in Amsterdam, now settled with children in Perth, had not been helpful, all things considered, the Dutchman said, he went on talking to himself when he wasn't talking directly to Delage, as if Delage wasn't there. "Not for a moment have I stopped being interested in my wife, if you know what I mean," he told Delage. "After our years together, it is a source of unhappiness to realize she is no longer interested in our situation, how we once were, what is left of it now. She has removed me entirely from the equation, all ideas of me." The Dutchman hardly noticed he had become saturated at the rail, any physical discomfort only reinforced his psychological discomfort. "You could have been swept overboard, and disappeared completely," Elisabeth said. "And then what would I do?" Delage was having difficulty keeping his balance, drying his hair with a towel. "What a question! I would expect you to immediately jump in and save me." "I do not know why you find him especially interesting," she went on, "his circumstances are not uncommon." "He has me worried.

He doesn't look in great shape. Whoopsie!" The ship was pitching and rolling. "The poor wife, think of her. She could have been driven crazy by him." "That's possible," Delage changing out of his trousers, "I wouldn't be surprised." "You have spent more time talking to him than talking to me," though she was not really complaining. Delage noticed she had been sighing less on the ship than on land. "I have added up the minutes," she looked up at the ceiling. Elisabeth envied the easy relationships between men, however slight. He removed the bones from the fish for her. She imagined an honesty, or simplicity between them, although she knew if she questioned Delage about it he would avoid a straight answer, it was not a subject he had given any thought to. On the small deck, the Dutchman talking, Delage saw how little he knew, only her shape, little more, waiting in his cabin, he was always on the brink of discovering more about her, her mother stood before him, he knew her even less, if he could say he knew her at all, yet he believed he understood the mother more than he did her daughter. Her breast in her hand, in the room, it was phosphorescent. Elisabeth smiled and sat up when he said Amalia reminded him of the Statue of Liberty, always standing. "But my mother could hardly be called passive. She has strong feelings about everything." "I think she is brave." "I do not know what you mean by that." "I like her very much." It was hard enough to know your own mother, let alone anybody else in the world. Elisabeth spoke of herself sparingly, indifferently, to an unusual extent, which made him all the more thoughtful, unlike his sister whether on the phone or in person, she invariably came out with everything possible about herself, everything she could think of, even when it had not yet happened. The two sisters emerged in similar charcoal gray, the discarded sister adding a series of silk scarves which featured horses, a promising touch, adding color to her mood, should anyone in the family be meeting the ship in Melbourne. All along they had hardly said hello to the Dutchman, almost ignoring his presence, some people don't have any manners, even in the narrow confines of a ship, it doesn't hurt to say "Good morning," or "Too rough for you?" although he seemed not to notice. The incomprehension of the discarded sister had stabilized, as a consequence the anger and weeping diminished, the younger one told Elisabeth, they were yet to return to their normal sisterly ease, she confided, visually the younger attentive one maintained what is called a supporting role, in Melbourne they lived ten minutes from each other, she would see to it that her discarded sister had plenty of people around her, while the husband was off somewhere pursuing a new life. There were the same large birds following the ship, then on the fourth day the sun came out. "The voyage had been the bookkeeper's idea, she made a strong case for it. But now here I am returning without the piano on board," he pulled out brochures advertising the Delage. "For all the difficulties, the trip has almost paid for itself. Everything saved is money earned. We have been having problems with the banks and cash flow. And, as our bookkeeper pointed out, I hadn't taken a day off in God knows how many years. She has made a big difference to the office. It's quite a professional outfit now. Before she arrived, the filing system, for example, was a terrible mess. She knows nothing about pianos, the craftsmanship that goes into them, and all that. Otherwise, she pretty well runs the company." When he left for Europe she was pregnant, the question was whether she would be staying in the job. "This is the woman from Slovakia?" Elisabeth had an uninterested air, turning the pages of the brochure, the Delage piano photographed from different angles, including an aerial view, featured pale glossy colors Delage had come to think were garish. "All along I was more interested in the workings of the piano than its appearance, which I know is the road to bankruptcy." The fine grain of the highly polished timbers, taken from forest trees on the verge of extinction, had shifted attention from the technical improvements hidden beneath the lid, which produced the Delage sound, a sound like no other piano sound. The range of colors reminded him of the garage-door man in Perth, his horizontal doors, which opened like enormous piano lids, came in eye-catching colors, the salesman had informed the Dutchman, although white was generally preferred. "Your mother said not to worry about the color. Apparently in a Vienna drawing room, a nicotine-brown or a white piano doesn't look out of place. I saw straightaway what she meant." It had been a long time since he had been out of the factory for more than a few days, separated from the people he had become accustomed to, their attitudes to him, the way they spoke, combed their hair, each with their own skills, stubbornnesses, the many encounters, solving problems together, his daily habits, on the streets, in the rooms where he slept and ate, each morning stepping out after shaving and reading the *Telegraph*, assembled into what felt like normal life, a slightly useful life. In fact, aside from when he came down years ago with the flu, just as the first piano was being finished, Frank Delage could not remember being away from the factory for more than a day. "In the early days there was a lot of problem-solving." It was the part he most enjoyed. "I'd sleep in the factory. I had a camp-stretcher made up in the corner," the thought of which sent Elisabeth, like others, into chortling. Not only had he been away now for six weeks, possibly more, perhaps seven, without newspapers, calendars, clocks on the ship, he had spent more time alone with Elisabeth von Schalla than he had with any woman before, establishing a separate layer of habit, with an inevitability he hardly thought about. "When we arrive, what was it you planned on doing?" He was looking thoughtful as he spoke. He had a responsibility, he had to be careful. After the Schalla palace in Vienna, she could easily take one look at his rented two-bedroom with balcony apartment in Artarmon, Sydney, and catch the first plane home. She kicked one leg up, "Back to *Wien*? I am sorry, that is no longer possible." Together they spent hours in the cabin or out on the deck, they were not always saying anything of note, at intervals settling into various kinds of silences, interesting, they were not at all uncomfortable, the occasional sighs from Elisabeth were more like breathing. The *Romance* had slowed outside Port Phillip Bay for the pilot. Delage watched as he climbed on board from the tiny unstable boat, a stocky bare-headed man wearing a nylon jacket and a tie. "Do you want some news? I don't have any," he said to Delage in passing, who had been waiting for the Dutchman—at other ports they had leaned together over the rail on the small deck, observing the pilots making grabs at the swinging ladder, difficult in rough weather. "It is easier getting on than getting off," the Dutchman had observed. The pilot gave Delage his folded newspaper after he had steered the ship through the Heads, and complained about the lack of dredging, it was making the entrance dangerous for the large ships. "It is an accident about to happen," Delage managed to hear over the wind and engines. How the complicated events of the world are compressed into sheets of paper always of the same size, which need to be filled to the outer edges every day, reports from long distances or eyewitness accounts taken on trust, reporting or prophesying situations which begin to change, as everything does, even as the newspaper is being printed, replaced the following day by a fresh set of happenings, or possibly about to happen, people described in victory or at a loss, or stories without people at all, a melting glacier, worth reading or at least perusing. News is essentially about other people's mistakes, or their misfortunes, a regular feature is the one-paragraph report of disaster in remote regions (floods, bushfires, earthquakes, train crashes, a building collapses, the obligatory tornado, overloaded ferry has sunk), the short efficient sentences produce an exclamatory effect whether intended or not. There will always be news whether there's any news or not. The finance, sports and weather pages can be relied upon more than any of the other pages. Anything to do with art, literature, music a matter of opinion in the newspapers, through which a consensus eventually may form, while the larger opinion pieces are just that, one thought laid out at a time, a man swinging a sledgehammer to erect a circus tent. Newspapers raise unimportant incidents to the level of important incidents. This was how Frank Delage, small manufacturer, read about his piano in Europe, and saw the photograph, not in the folded tabloid the pilot had handed him as he left the ship, another newspaper a few days later, on the way to Sydney. Whenever he thought of Konrad von Schalla and his outspoken words, often he did, he thought of von Schalla's wife at arm's length, he had almost reached out to her but had not, he had but not enough. He should have, he had begun to, but had not. Thinking of Elisabeth, he would return to thinking of her mother, Amalia, the small similarities, mother in the daughter, which made her attraction intimate. Elisabeth had a solemnity that was casual, modern. In his short time in Vienna, he had become drawn into the Schalla family, for different reasons each of them wanted his presence, he, from Sydney not Vienna, an entirely fresh face, musical, yet not musical at all, not by their standards, at the most inconvenient times with Elisabeth he would think of her mother in Vienna, Amalia von Schalla, standing, she appeared before him, it was difficult, if not impossible, to avoid. At the last minute the captain announced the ship was having six hours turnaround, and would leave on the tide before midnight, which allowed Delage and Elisabeth only a quick tour of the city from a taxi. The two sisters with their suitcases at the top of the gangway were in such a hurry to leave the ship and have Melbourne, marvelous

Melbourne, underfoot, family and friends waiting on the wharf under umbrellas, they said goodbye hurriedly, looking at the wharf and away at the skyline, office towers lit up, rather than at Delage and Elisabeth; the sisters were eager yet awkward, the older rejected sister appeared as a young or youngish widow in black, except for a small rosella parrot brooch, avoiding Delage and Elisabeth entirely, not a glance in their direction, already she was wary about her new life in Elwood, Melbourne, how she would be seen, her sister providing support nearby, which she wanted but didn't want at all, all of which gave Delage and Elisabeth the opposite feelings, tolerance, energy, optimism, curiosity. Delage left it up to the taxi driver to show them the sights of Melbourne, in richness and so forth a city closer to Sydney, certainly than to Perth, Singapore, Port Said, he was from Riga, "that's in Latvia," he said, not everybody knew, a man with large sloping shoulders, "I wouldn't go back to Riga if my grandmother was on fire. There is always something wrong with a city, your only hope is to choose one with the smallest number of faults." Every place where people had settled, congregated, built and added their monuments and decorations, had its faults. By not saying anything, trying instead to make sense of the shapes in the darkness, Delage and Elisabeth appeared to give encouragement to the driver who reeled off the major cities in the world and their most unattractive characteristics, he had been to all of them, he said, beginning with Riga, which had no personality whatsoever, and a terrible sewerage system, Vienna and Sydney each had so many things wrong it was difficult to know where to begin. "There are irritable people everywhere," Delage leaned into Elisabeth, "even in Melbourne." Whenever the driver from Riga described the faults of another city his sloping shoulders shook with what could only be satisfaction. At least Melbourne had a river. In the darkness it wandered like a sunken road, lights reflected and stretched on the surface. Government House was behind the bushes. There was the Olympic swimming pool, the Melbourne Cricket Ground in silhouette. Unfortunately the taxi was fogging up. The rain had almost stopped. On the way back, they passed the concert hall and the art gallery, one an enormous gray horizontal box, the other a circular shape, more or less brought together by an Eiffel Tower structure of welded pipes, painted glossy white. With the six-hour turnaround they would not be flying to Sydney, Delage's idea, it would take just a few days more by ship, following the east coast of Australia. These were among their happiest days. They now had the small deck to themselves, Elisabeth reclining in her large sunglasses, as if there were no sunlight back in Austria, or anywhere else in Europe, her breast, Delage noted, slightly rounder than her mother's, filling his hand, Delage flipping through the newspaper he'd bought in Melbourne, without knowing why, Australian newspapers are amongst the worst in the world, certainly the worst in the English-speaking world, Australian journalists practice a violent simplicity which has been successfully exported to the rest of the English-speaking world, others who are called broadsheet or quality journalists, said to be the level-headed ones, are hardly better with their embarrassing self-importance, making pronouncements concerning the world with the self-assurance of the airport taxi driver—before long they'll be on television making their pronouncements, replacing the actual newsmakers, it would eventually infect the thinking capacity of those who consume Australian newspapers. Delage wondered why he had bought the newspaper, he was complaining to Elisabeth about them, about the general situation of his country, who was listening, but Elisabeth never read newspapers, which explained her untroubled appearance, her smooth skin tone, still talking, an audience at least of one, he turned to the inside of the national daily, Saturday edition, a paper he didn't normally read. Elisabeth opened her eyes, he had stopped talking. The pianist was a young woman with long black hair, on stage naked, playing the piano while it was burning in different places, it had been set alight, while an accompanist in a tuxedo swinging an axe, a sledgehammer and rubber mallet set about destroying it, at rhythmic intervals to a score, the only Delage concert grand in Europe smashed into little pieces, until it was not a piano at all, and there was no music possible, nothing left to go on, only the beginning of silence, before an audience in formal evening wear, the premiere performance of what was an avant-garde work by the Austrian composer, Paul Hildebrand, in Vienna last week.

Pleased to introduce Elisabeth to Sydney, Delage talking over his shoulder, making the best of his situation, of his many difficulties, deploying here the salesman's expansive manner, he was on home turf, near enough, Botany Bay being a suburb of Sydney, Elisabeth had dressed for serious walking, silk scarf, brown flat shoes, still on his sea-legs, he slipped on the last step of the gangway where there was a gap to the wharf, fell headfirst onto the concrete. There had been no sign of the Dutchman, he must have disembarked, Delage wrote a note giving his Sydney address, Elisabeth slid it under the cabin door. As Delage lay on the wharf, his first thought was the pianos, the storage room between the office and the factory floor could be used to display the pianos under bright lights, instead of having them under wraps in a corner waiting for delivery, an idea worth putting to the Slovakian bookkeeper. Only a few people are interested in many different ideas. It is natural that a person's most attractive qualities appeal only to a narrow range of others. Delage was left wondering if Elisabeth von Schalla now saw him as a weakened man, not to be relied upon, all too ordinary once seen in his own surroundings. From now on he was going to concentrate on the home market. One day he might go back to Vienna, just for a visit. Elisabeth was bending over, repeating his name. "The world changes slowly, too slowly," from behind his minuscule desk, von Schalla hardly moved his lips, a man of experience, if ever there was, to Delage the world was slowly changing before him, he slowly thought it. He was happy to remain face down for a moment to gather his wits, before clearing his throat and getting to his feet, he grabbed at Elisabeth's shoulder, aware of the German captain and some of the officers looking down at him. "I don't know what went wrong there," sensing he had become a slightly different person, now standing on firm ground, though still holding her shoulder.

MURRAY BAIL was born in Adelaide in 1941 and now lives in Sydney. His fiction, which includes *Eucalyptus*, *Holden's Performance*, *Homesickness* and *The Drover's Wife and Other Stories*, has been translated into more than twenty-five languages. *Eucalyptus* was the winner of the Commonwealth Writers' Prize and the Miles Franklin Literary Award.